Jean Chapman began her writing career as a freelance journalist before going on to write fiction. Her books have been shortlisted for both the Scottish Book Trust Award and the RNA Major Award, and she is the three-time President of the Leicester Writers' Club.

A WATERY GRAVE

Out on a morning run, ex-Met officer John Cannon vaults a stile, becomes ensnared in a discarded fishing line — and entangled in trouble. For there is a macabre discovery at the far end of this line, leading John into a search for a missing au pair, which puts him into conflict with the local police and involvement with international crime. He discovers that the local Health Spa has much to conceal, with its security guards and dogs patrolling the grounds. But the Portuguese owner is a ruthless businessman, and Cannon faces danger every step of the way . . .

JEAN CHAPMAN

◆

A
WATERY GRAVE

Complete and Unabridged

ULVERSCROFT
Leicester

First published in Great Britain in 2011 by
Robert Hale Limited
London

First Large Print Edition
published 2012
by arrangement with
Robert Hale Limited
London

British Library CIP Data

Chapman, Jean, *1929 –*
   A watery grave.
   1. Ex-police officers- -Great Britain- -Fiction. 2. Missing
   persons- -Investigation- -Great Britain- -Fiction.
   3. Detective and mystery stories. 4. Large type books.
   I. Title
   823.9′14–dc23

   ISBN 978–1–4448–1062–2

Published by
F. A. Thorpe (Publishing)
Anstey, Leicestershire

Set by Words & Graphics Ltd.
Anstey, Leicestershire
Printed and bound in Great Britain by
T. J. International Ltd., Padstow, Cornwall

This book is printed on acid-free paper

1

Cannon took a last deep invigorating breath of the air blowing straight in from the North Sea, then turned his back on the broad expanse of ocean to run inland.

He was returning from a morning jog to his Fenland public house with new enthusiasm. He felt elated because at long last he and his partner, Liz, had put long held plans into action — the builders were in.

The conversion of their old stable block into guest rooms had been blessed by the planning authorities, and so far the local builder he had given the job to, had been exemplary. His men were on time, and apart from lunch-breaks the men — two of whom he understood were new — had worked well. Archie Burns had been around every single day of these first weeks, making sure the work was being done to his high standards, and the site left tidy every evening.

'Plenty of time for it all to go wrong,' Alan Hoskins, the public house's best customer, had assured him, with that air the old man had of knowing far more than he was telling.

'Good old Hoskins, always last out — often

1

first in,' Cannon muttered as he ran towards a low fence, which he prepared to vault in his usual way. But as he tried to lift his front foot he found all he was able to do was throw his arms out to prevent himself crashing face-first into the stile — for his feet were suddenly entangled in something — something very strong and totally disabling. He could move neither foot, and, when he saw what held him, he was not surprised: he was entangled in a discarded fishing line.

The fine strong gut was caught not just around his shoes, but pulled tight under the metal eyelets and entangled in the laces of his trainers. He tried to balance and free himself and it all became worse. In the end he sat down, took off one trainer at a time and began painstakingly to unravel the mess. Someone it seemed had discarded a full reel of fishing line, which was now endangering any man or beast which came this way. Cannon was angry for the milking-cows at the far side of this pasture land. He judged it would be the same kind of person who discarded the split lead-shot used as fishing weights, for ducks and geese to peck up, with fatal results.

Both shoes free he put them back on and began to gather up the gut in an untidy ball, following it along the hedgerow. He did think of getting out his pocket-knife and cutting the line, but his conscience would not allow that. He would gather up every last millimetre and take it home to dispose of safely — so on he went, thinking whatever had laid this trail — for such it began to feel like — must have crawled along on its belly to entangle it in as many roots and branches as possible. He hoped he was not going to find some unfortunate wild creature at the other end. And he must surely be nearing the end; he already had quite a ball in his hands, and had reached a point where a minor road ran the other side of the hedge. Someone had undoubtedly thrown the tangled mass over into the field, and some other unwitting being, two- or four-footed, had become entangled, as he had, and carried it along the hedgerow.

He gave the line a good jerk but it resisted so sharply it cut into the middle crease of his fingers, making three of them bleed.

'Damn it!' He tried to ball the springy gut tighter, besmirching the lot with his blood as he tried. The tension on the line was certainly not slacking off. Some fish, he thought.

Then abruptly the line plunged to the left down into a conduit, a gully dug deep to drain water from the roadway when wind and tide pushed the sea inland — and he finally saw what held the gut so firmly.

'For Christ's sake!' he exclaimed. A man lay there, on his face, his hands and arms raised above his head as if he tried to cling to the grasses and reeds that had grown strong and tall from the sides and bottom of the gully. He could see that the line he had collected ended here — beneath this man — somewhere . . .

Cannon was aware he talked to the man, though he looked beyond earthly help — but Cannon had to be sure, life could be nurtured from the tiniest spark if help came in time. He could see if he tried to reach from above he might well slip on top of the man, so going a little further along he jumped over into the concealed, overgrown, depths of the gully. It was deeper than he expected and pushing back through the growth of weeds he found his waist was now level with the outstretched form.

As he lifted a hand to feel for a pulse in the neck, there was movement. Cannon's heart leapt as for one moment he thought the man had been sleeping and now turned to see who disturbed him, but the movement was no more than displacement and the angle of the gully turned the man as he slid down, so he came to rest, face-up — on Cannon's feet. A man inexperienced with death — and murder

— might have panicked, leapt and run, but, though his heart pounded, Cannon froze into an observation machine — and there was much to take in.

First the weight across his feet was that of a dead man, dead weight, the heaviness of a corpse with no air in his lungs had for years been a working reality for Cannon.

Now he was face up, Cannon saw that the face and hair were plastered with so much black Fen mud, he could have been wearing one of those face-packs he had occasionally been startled to find Liz wearing. Cannon stooped to look beneath the chin, and saw the other end of the fishing line, doubled over, and used as a garrotte.

The gut had cut deep into the flesh, so deeply the neck had almost closed over it, sealing off any great flow of blood. Death, Cannon knew, would have been swift, though what had happened to this man before he died was another matter, for though his features and much of his dark hair were thickly coated with mud, his clothes looked clean, his black shoes were immaculate enough for a company boardroom.

Cannon sighed heavily — like any other member of the public, he did not want this involvement — he just wanted to get on with his life. With the utmost delicacy he inched his feet back until they were free of the weight, then reached for his mobile phone, tapped in the number of the local constabulary, and, as it was answered, recognized the voice on the other end.

'Sergeant Maddern?' he queried.

'Is it John Cannon?' a cheerful voice asked in reply.

'It is, Sergeant, and I've just found a body . . . '

There was a noise that almost sounded like a choked-off laugh. 'What, one of Hoskins' victims? What's he poached now, fish, fowl or larger beast?' When there was no immediate reply the sergeant's manner changed, 'You're not serious?'

His story told, he felt the local sergeant knew where he was better than he did himself. 'You'll be next to Three Gates Marsh on the St Andrew's Road,' he said, then asked, 'and you'll wait for our people?'

Cannon confirmed he would wait, and as he paused before ringing Liz, he had a sudden feeling of total desolation, of impending personal disaster. He tried to convince himself it was just the whining of the wind through the reeds, a mournful noise in an otherwise silent landscape, as if the elements keened for the departed — whoever the departed was.

He took a long hard look at the face before he climbed out of the gully. The mouth was open and full of mud, the nostrils completely clogged. No breath had struggled in and out of that mouth or those nostrils; the man had been dead before his face and head had become thick-coated with mud. So had he been garrotted, then thrown into one of the many drains that cut through the land straight to the sea, drains, twenty, thirty and forty feet deep? And if he had, why fish him out, and dress him with all the care of an undertaker preparing a deceased for grieving relatives to view — yet leave the face so obscured?

Cannon shuddered. Long experience in the Met never quite prepared him for the strange and bizarre where crime was concerned. He added his own sigh to the whining wind as he punched in Liz's number.

'John?' she queried his call, 'What's wrong?'

As he told her he realized how sticky his phone was, and saw his fingers were still bleeding. He thought ironically that he had more blood about himself than the body had, and then something else happened — as he stared down at the man's face while he talked to Liz, a neat half of the mud on the upturned face dropped away as neatly as a mould from a cast. 'My God,' he breathed, 'I know him.'

'John!' Liz exclaimed, 'John, who is it?'

'It's one of those two new builders who've been working on our stables, the taller one with the black wavy-hair.'

'Nick,' she said, and before he could answer she asked, 'So is Stefan there?'

'I've seen no one else.'

'They're always together,' she added. 'Do you think something's happened to him?'

He glanced all around and along the road to where it swept inland and he could see a flashing pin-point of blue light, and faintly, for the wind was blowing the sound away from him, hear a siren. For some reason he remembered Alan Hoskins's comment the first time he had seen the two dark haired men. 'They're no more builders than I'm landed gentry,' he had said.

'The police are nearly here,' he told Liz, 'I'll keep you posted.'

Nick and Stefan. Cannon had wondered if Stefan was an illegal immigrant, though it would be unlike the straight-laced Archie Burns to do anything outside the law. But Stefan's pump-water-straight black hair, pitch-black eyes, his stilted English and his accent had suggested Croatia to Cannon, while Nick had been a Londoner, able to talk to anyone on any subject. Cannon had twice had to intervene when Nick had sparked a bar-room debate on some news item, which had threatened to get less than good-natured. Nick had been an opinionated young man.

The pair had been an unlikely combination. Cannon wondered if they had spent all their free time together; they had bought lunches in the pub everyday since the work started. Cannon had expected them to bring their own pack-ups, eat in the stables, but there had been an odd closeness about these two, as if they shared not just a bar meal, but a secret. Cannon stared down at the murdered young man and remembered it always had been Nick who had paid.

There was no more time to ponder as the sound of the siren came closer, the blue light flashed on the other side of the hedge. He waved his arms to attract attention; brakes screeched as the car came to a halt, car doors opened and were slammed to.

Cannon was pleased to see Sergeant Maddern was one of the men; he was a person who gave confidence to the troubled just by his presence. The other in plain clothes would undoubtedly be the new detective inspector he had heard of but not so far met. 'With you in a moment, John,' Maddern called, adding to the inspector, 'there's a gate back a few yards.'

The first words Cannon heard the inspector say were preceded by a loud suck between his front teeth. 'Detective Inspector Jones,' he introduced himself, 'Maddern's told me who you are,' he said as he approached the culvert and looked down at the dead man.

'I do know who the man is now . . . ' Cannon began.

'Now?' Jones queried.

'The wind must have dried the mud, and as you see it's fallen away from half of the face.'

'And?'

'He's one of the builders who've been working on my stable conversion,' Cannon said.

'You've touched nothing?'

'Well . . . '

'So you have?' The question snapped in like a whiplash, and when the explanation did not seem to please, the teeth were sucked once more. 'The scene of crime supervisor is not going to be pleased with you,' Jones added, then giving the nod to the Sergeant added, 'get on to the CSI, the sooner they're here the better. Meanwhile Mr Cannon can tell me about this fishing line,' the inspector looked down at the ball of gut at their feet, adding, 'and the blood on it.'

Cannon opened his hand to show the cut fingers. 'I tried to pull it free . . . ' He stopped as the inspector sucked at his teeth again. Cannon thought he should be told about the habit before some Saturday night drunk took exception and rid him of his teeth permanently.

Sergeant Maddern who had been on his mobile radio reported that their crime scene investigators would be there asap.

'I should have been back at my pub some time ago,' Cannon began, knowing the unspoken appeal to be allowed to go was unlikely to be heard.

'You will have rung on your mobile,' the inspector stated.

'Yes, but I do have work to do . . . '

The inspector gave him a withering look, then said, 'While we wait, you can show me where you first tangled with this line. Sergeant, see nothing and no one touches anything.'

By the time they stood at the stile looking toward *The Trap*, Cannon had found little to like in this inspector, who communicated by sucks and grunts as much as words. He asked what Cannon thought had carried the line all the way to where they stood. Cannon speculated it could have been a fox, lucky to rid itself of the wretched stuff. 'Perhaps,' he added, 'it freed itself when it pushed under the stile.'

'It would have been better, if it had still been here — dead or alive,' the inspector said with a cold calculating look at Cannon and a suck at his teeth.

Why wait for a Saturday night drunk, Cannon wondered.

They walked back and still the CSI people had not showed. 'Sergeant Maddern can take a preliminary statement,' the inspector conceded, nodding in the direction of the police car.

The CSI van arrived just as he and Sergeant Maddern were settled in the back of the police car. 'Keep your head down,' Sergeant Jim Maddern advised. 'Don't give him a chance to stop us getting this over. You'll be wanting to get back to Liz.'

'Right,' Cannon agreed, feeling he had an ally in the hefty Sergeant, though why he should feel he needed one was an irritation.

By the time the statement was made, signed and he climbed from the car, men in white suits had taped off large areas both sides of the hedge, a photographer was already busy, and there was some discussion about covering the crime scene CSI had identified as necessary, lying as it did on both sides of the hedge. Cannon walked back past the men, noting that the ball of fishing line now lay on top of the body, ready to be moved with it.

These men took no notice of Cannon; as Sergeant Maddern said, they 'don't do people', they were forensics pure and simple. Cannon was walking away, keen to be home, to talk to Liz, to see if Stefan was on site, when a phone burbled out an insistent and rising musical jingle, demanding attention. Cannon stopped walking and for a second everyone froze, as they identified where the sound was coming from, and all focussed on the body in the ditch.

Cannon knew it would not be answered, there was nothing anyone on site would be able, or allowed, to tell the caller, but the tension visibly relaxed when the phone stopped. 'I want the caller traced, fast, Franklyn,' Jones said.

'Of course,' the CSI manager, so abruptly addressed told him, adding, 'and I'd like you back a good fifty yards.'

Cannon once more retraced the path of the fishing line with Jones and Franklyn, this time much further from the hedgerow than before, to preserve any evidence Cannon — and Jones — had not already disturbed.

'We'll need more of your men for a

fingertip search along here, and to guard the site until we've finished,' Franklyn said.

Jones grunted.

Cannon was pleased the finer points of etiquette between police and other departments were no longer his worry, and he prepared to move away, lifting a hand to indicate a piece of fencing he could climb without using the stile Franklyn was poring over, hands clasped behind his back in true professorial manner.

'I'll come with you,' Jones said, and radioed his sergeant to pick him up at The Trap.

Cannon had anticipated sprinting the rest of the way, but now he was compelled to walk he studied the detective, automatically going down the professional list of observation details: height, medium; build, medium, though the face was broader and fatter than the figure might have suggested and the eyes were small and deep-set. A middle-aged detective, in well worn-in navy trousers and anorak. 'Where are you from, Inspector,' he asked.

'North Yorkshire,' Jones replied, 'way back. And you?'

'My father was a cockney barrow-boy,' he answered.

'I know your Met history, and your partner's,' Jones went on. 'She was badly hurt

14

in a gang conflict. You brought them all to justice — and resigned.' The last word held a rising note of inquiry, but Cannon felt no need to justify his actions. It had felt right at the time and when he thought of Liz, still did.

What he had not expected as he ushered Jones in through the back porch, was perfect peace and quiet. There was no sound anywhere. He led the way through to the kitchen, then to the bar, then to the stairs and called, 'Liz, you there?'

'Outside somewhere,' Jones suggested.

Cannon did not answer, forcing down the rising panic which still assailed him when Liz was not where he expected her to be, a legacy of the case Jones had touched on. He led the way along the flower-decked white front of the pub. The tubs and hanging baskets were already planted with blue, yellow and purple pansies, mixed with variegated ivies, to give colour to autumn and the fast approaching winter months.

He paused in the archway to the stable-yard and called again. Liz immediately came out of the old harness room nearest to him, a mobile phone to her ear.

Before Cannon could speak Jones demanded, 'Who are you phoning?'

She paused and very deliberately pushed her long blonde hair over her shoulder with her free hand. 'You must be our new inspector,' she said.

He sucked his teeth, grunted and nodded at the mobile.

'I was not calling anyone,' she said, 'Archie Burns, our builder has just phoned in.'

'So you told him?'

'He wanted to know if Nick and Stefan were already here. I told him what I knew, then came to check whether Stefan was here, while he hung on — '

'And?' Jones snapped, 'and . . . ?'

'We are not still in the force,' Cannon interrupted, 'just assisting with your inquiries.'

Liz shook her head at Cannon, his reaction hardly likely to help, and answered Jones. 'There is no one here, Archie Burns has been to the flat the two men share, and there was no one there — well no one answered the door.'

'So is this Archie Burns coming here?'

'No, they have a family panic on, their daughter and grand-children coming on an unexpected visit from Australia,' Liz told them. 'Mr Burns had taken the men's wages to where they live in case he doesn't manage to get over here today, his wife — '

'I'll need the address of their flat,' Jones interrupted, 'where's his office?'

'At his house,' Cannon said, 'and his wife does his office work.'

Jones grunted, but lost no time talking on his mobile to his sergeant. 'Pick me up,' he said abruptly, 'now.'

Cannon raised his eyebrows at Liz, who pointedly ignored him.

'So what do you know about these two workmen?' the inspector went on, following Liz as she made her way to the pub kitchen.

'The two of them occasionally came back here in the evenings,' she said as she made mugs of tea, 'quite late usually, and I had the impression they had been somewhere else and were calling here before they went home, though until Mr Burns rang I had no idea they lived together.' She glanced at Cannon, 'I've no idea what their surnames are. Have you, John?'

Cannon gave a negative grunt.

'Stefan,' Jones went on, 'a foreign name, illegal worker do you think?'

'Burns wouldn't employ anyone with dodgy papers, he's straight as a die,' Cannon said.

'I wonder if I could ask you if you have a room upstairs which gives a view of the land towards the sea,' Jones asked.

'I have a room and a telescope,' Cannon heard himself say. Liz grinned at his sudden capitulation.

Upstairs in their private quarters John led the inspector to their sitting room where his prized brass telescope stood mounted in the window.

'Bird watcher?' Jones asked.

'Bird watcher and admirer, ever since I came to live here,' Cannon replied. 'I felt greeted by birds.'

Jones sucked his teeth, but seated himself behind the telescope. 'This is some instrument,' he admitted, with some warmth in his voice at last. 'Some sweep of coast, and a good view of the murder site.' He swung the telescope from north to east, quietly grunting and sucking his teeth from time to time.

'Inspector,' Liz called from downstairs, 'your lift's here.'

'Interesting,' Jones said as he straightened, 'more water than land.'

'Yes, you have to watch your step out here,' Cannon said.

'Oh! I always do, landlord, I always do.'

They watched him go. 'I've know young policemen leave the force because they've encountered an ignorant — like that. Bet he calls the young constables 'lad'.'

Liz hooked her hand through his arm. 'You're probably right, but who do you think has murdered that young man, not Stefan surely, they were friends — but where is he?'

2

The fate of one of their young builders, the absence of the other, the total silence in the stables, made Cannon and Liz absent-minded about the daily routines. It was not until they heard pounding on their front door that they realized morning opening time had arrived.

Local lorry drivers who were regular callers for Liz's breakfasts on their way home from delivering local produce to all parts of the UK were agog with their sightings of white-suited figures, blue and white tape and the tent. John and Liz told and retold the story, both automatically omitting the bizarre details — the muddied face, the clean clothes and spotless shoes. Though having admitted how he came to find the body, Cannon noted that most took a morbid interest in his plastered fingers.

Hoskins wanted to know all the details when he came in that evening, but then, true to what John knew of him when there was real trouble, sat watchful and quiet in his usual seat soaking in discussion and speculation.

It was only minutes to last orders, when the

tall lean figure of Archie Burns came almost uncertainly into the bar, and Hoskins became more alert in his pew seat next to the counter.

Cannon wondered if the builder brought more bad news, for his usual amiable expression was missing, new lines of worry creased his cheeks and brow. He looked considerably older than his sixty years, fussed and uncomfortable in a dark, tweed, Sunday-best, suit.

'All right? What will you have?' Cannon asked, adding, 'a brandy, on the house.'

'No, just a half of bitter,' he replied.

'The inspector been to see you?' Cannon asked.

Burns nodded.

'He caught you at home?'

'Yes,' he confirmed, then added with a break in his voice, 'we're going to Heathrow tonight . . . to meet my daughter and the grandchildren . . . '

'It's not good news, your daughter coming?' Cannon asked, alarmed by Archie's expression.

He shook his head. 'Wife finally managed to speak to her on a computer link up at the Aussie airport,' he paused seeming to have to summon energy to continue, 'not just marriage break-up, but there's the grandchildren crying their eyes out because they are leaving their Daddy behind.'

Liz, who had joined them, raised the counter flap.

'Come through,' she said.

Burns nodded his thanks and did as he was told. Liz went with him, leaving John to see the last customers away and lock up.

'Bad business,' Hoskins said, as Cannon followed him outside and waited while he retrieved his bicycle from inside the stable archway. The old man suddenly stopped, shook his head violently, 'All this wilful leaving of each other, ruining lives. If they knew how final the last parting is, and when you yearn to have things back the way they were, and how all your tears and all your longings, won't ever bring them back and make it the same, they might think, not twice, but a couple of hundred times before they split up, break hearts.' With that he swung his leg over his cross bar and rode away, a little faster than his usual speed.

Cannon stood as he often did and watched the bike's antiquated rear-light dwindle into the darkness. Tonight he wondered how long Hoskins had been on his own. Some time ago a faded photograph of a young Hoskins in army uniform with a young bride on his arm, had fallen from his wallet on to the counter. Cannon remembered the old man scooping it up and replacing it with trembling fingers. Then one evening in the bar some of the locals had discussed whether or not they were right to think he had once had a daughter, but they were too young to remember and the conversation had stopped when the man in question had walked in. Cannon realized what a lot they did not know about Hoskins as he locked and bolted the front doors.

In the kitchen Liz was pouring tea.

'So how is Mrs Burns taking all this?' he queried.

'Badly.' Archie said, shaking his head, eyes lowered to the table. 'Neither of us expected this, all the messages, the computer contacts where we could see each other, there's been no clue . . . none that we picked up anyway.' He paused and looked up at Liz, 'I wonder if we didn't just want to believe everything was all right, either that, or our Joy was too good at hiding her troubles.' He took the mug of tea Liz had poured. 'But I needn't burden you with all this, but coming on top of this murder . . . I feel I've been hit with a pole axe . . . and that inspector . . . ' Archie again paused and shook his head.

'Didn't help,' Cannon suggested.

'No, he made me feel as if whatever had happened was my fault.'

Cannon nodded. 'It's a special gift he has,' he said.

'I gave him the address of the flat where the men lived, but . . . '

'We've heard they found no one there,' Liz said.

'No, he came to my home, but the wife had gone to her sister's to arrange about beds and things. He tried to find her, but seems they had decided to go out and buy bunk beds. He wanted all the paperwork, all the details I have about Stefan . . . and Nick, which the wife deals with. I told him I'd let him have them as soon as the wife came home. I wondered if I could leave this with you,' he paused to push his hand into his inside pocket and brought out a sealed envelope. 'I don't want to have to see that inspector again. I'll telephone him and tell him it's with you.'

'I could do that,' Cannon said, taking the envelope as Archie rose.

'No, I think that's my job. You've been kind enough as it is,' he said, adding, 'which makes me feel worse because I have to say I'm not sure when I can start work on your conversion again. I may need to set on more men.'

'You worry about your family first,' Liz said. 'Plenty of time when this is all behind us.' She smiled ruefully at John as they followed Archie to the door. He grimaced back, acknowledging that life seemed to have a habit of kicking their plans into touch.

When they had seen Archie off, Liz picked up the envelope and put it on the dresser among the blue and white plates. 'A temptation?' John suggested.

'Well, yes,' Liz said pulling the band from her ponytail and releasing her long blonde hair, 'but I am quite sure the first thing Inspector Jones will do, is look to see if it has been tampered with.'

John sucked loudly through his teeth.

'You're a terrible man,' she told him, laughed briefly, then added, 'not sure whether I feel sorrier for Stefan or for Archie Burns, problems never come singly they say.'

Cannon lay awake, long after Liz slept, puzzling over the two young builders — and he kept remembering the envelope downstairs. In the end he slipped from their bed and crept downstairs, not putting on any lights until he reached the kitchen, here he silently closed the door, took the envelope from the dresser, turned it over in his hands. It was well sealed, with the Inspector's name written on the front. He put the kettle on, though he knew the old trick of steaming a letter open always left tell-tale crinkles. He was wrong to even think of doing such a thing, he knew that Liz would be furious.

He went to the back door, unlocked it and stepped out into a night full of moonlight, and stars that were overwhelmingly beautiful, brilliant in the dark landscape, where no street lights, no house lights, except his own intruded. He heard the kettle click off as he closed the door behind him and walked out beyond the side of the pub to see more, identifing some of the constellations: the close three-starred belt of Orion; the five bright stars making the 'W' shape of Casseopia; the seven stars of The Plough, in the shape of a ladle and its other name The Big Dipper.

He looked over towards the fields, could make out the white of the tent in the bright night, then turning back to the darkness of the buildings something caught his attention from the stables. A light? Yet the only opening to the back of the stables was the first-floor loading bay into the loft, used when hay was pitchforked straight up from a wagon. Perhaps a trick of his eyes, indigestion perhaps — but it had not been that kind of light. This had been more like a torch, a yellowish beam.

Cannon went as quickly and as quietly as he could to the front of the property, and once more through the archway into the stable yard, to the room below the hayloft. Even in the gloom of indoors he could see the builder's ladder had been pushed up through the trapdoor. He moved quietly to the ladder and heard his own cautious footsteps repeated overhead, someone was up there — and had heard him.

'Is that you, Stefan?' he called.

There was a second's silence then came a movement, a scurrying — Cannon thought of rats — but then there was a muted human-sounding exclamation, a thud . . .

Cannon was on the rungs, climbing, though the nearer the top he reached the more cautious he became, feeling increasingly like a target about to pop up in a fairground shooting booth. The smell of decades of disturbed hay dust reached him as, ready to duck at the slightest sound, he raised his head through the trapdoor. Nothing. Silence. He ventured further and could see that something dark obscured the night sky to the bottom right of the open loading-bay, something — or someone — crouching there.

'Don't be a fool,' he advised. 'It's John Cannon, I'm coming up.'

He did slowly. Anyone who had been in the loft for a time would probably see quite well, and he raised both hands. 'All right?' he asked, and took a step forward, which gave him a view of the fields, and of a moving shadow. Someone was nearly halfway across the field going towards the marshes and the sea, running, sometimes tripping, but struggling up and running on as if his life lay in his escape — perhaps it did. Cannon knew he had no chance of catching the man.

He reached over to the object in the doorway. It was a jacket, firmly caught on a nail protruding from the rotting frame. He held it up into the moonlight and thought he recognized it as one he had seen Stefan wearing. He had felt little doubt in any case that the figure who was now out of sight beyond the far hedge was the murdered man's companion.

If the two men had only worked for Archie for a few weeks then their flat and The Trap could be the only places Stefan knew well. Cannon was sure Stefan had not been in the country long, there was something in the way he watched and listened to everything and everybody, as if it was all strange to him. He was going to be a lost man without Nick, who surely he could not have murdered in such a bizarre and cold-blooded way. No, Cannon shook his head, 'and certainly not on his own,' he added aloud. He wondered where Stefan had been when the police raided the flat?

He carried the jacket back into the kitchen. In the outside pockets he found a very large old-fashioned red and white spotted handkerchief, an equally ancient pocket knife with a foreign maker's name on the bone handle, and several foreign coins, a Dutch guilder, two five kuna coins with the brown bear depicted on the reverse. Cannon knew these were Croatian. It was in the inside pocket that he found several folded papers, and a photograph together with two letters in a plain envelope.

He studied the photograph first. It was of a young woman, perhaps twenty, no more. She had black hair, which was rolled up in some way to form a kind of halo around her head, the style struck him as of someone who had to cut and care for her own hair. Her dress too, a pretty cotton flowered thing, frills at neck and sleeve edges, looked home-made. Respectable impoverishment, were the words that came to his mind, as he stared at the pleasant broad face, very dark eyes, an outdoor complexion, a smallish rose-bud mouth, just slightly opening as if she had been about to speak.

He opened out the pages the photo had been folded in. Letters they certainly were, handwritten in a language which to Cannon looked like a cross between Serbian and Latin, with Stefan's name at the beginning and a girl's name, Antonija, at the end of each one.

Laying them side by side, although neither were dated, one was obviously of much earlier origin, for the creases and crumpled state of the paper suggested it had been read and re-read. Below the girl's signature on the newer letter, was a short sentence which had the last word underlined several times.

The last sheets of paper were written in a different hand. Cannon's interest heightened as he saw at the top of each were the words, 'For Nick'. The next moment he was reaching for the letters and putting them alongside what increasingly looked like English translations of the two letters from Antonija.

The transcript of the earlier read:

Dear Stefan,

I trust all is well at home, and pray that the harvest will be good this year, and you and father not too tired at the end.

I am sorry the money I am able to send back is so much less than I thought, so little it is not worth what I have to put up with. These 'good' English people know I dare not complain as I am an illegal, so pay wages with deductions for food and lodgings. I think my wages must work out at about £2 per hour. I know this is wrong, but I have had luck. I meet a fellow, Ivo, in a pub in Boston where a lot of our people meet. Some are earning five and six times what I am, but Ivo has promised to put me

in touch with an agency, where I can earn very, very, much more — so I live in hope of better things.
Give all my love,
Your sister, Antonija

The second letter was shorter and much more urgent in tone, though again there was no date, just the fact that the paper was in better condition suggested it was written not too long ago.

Stefan, dear brother,
Help me, if you can. I am kept like a prisoner, but there is a man who cleans the windows, he will post this for me I pray. I have stolen money to give him.
Stefan, no good man will want me now. I think I will never see you or any of our family again, and many times I wish for death.
You must not blame yourself for any of this, I too thought it was a good idea.
Your loving sister, Antonija
If you could come you might save me.

It was the words 'come' and 'save' that were underlined four times.

Cannon's jaw clenched as he imagined that appeal landing in a caring family. Stefan, the loving brother, would have responded immediately. Cannon could imagine the journey, thumbed lifts, cheap buses through Slovakia to Germany and then Amsterdam, boat, lorry to this country — and to this particular part of the Fens — to try to rescue his sister.

And Nick? Where did Nick fit in? Cannon picked up the translations again. Nick had wanted these. Why? And why should Stefan bother to get a literal translation done for his friend?

The strange thing was that Cannon felt of the two, it was Nick who was more out of his normal sphere than the immigrant Stefan, who obviously had some building skills. Nick had been such a well-informed, articulate, young man, but had seemed more like a man who worked out in a gym than one used to hard manual labour.

As Cannon pondered he felt the familiar stirrings of an instinct he had developed during his service with the Metropolitan Police, an excitement that made him breathe faster, a knowledge that what was already known and visible, was only the tip of a big iceberg.

To untangle the logic of the twisted mind that had conceived this murder would need much thought, detailed analysis and investigation. He would have relished the task; he was going to hate handing this all over to Jones. He took up the original letters again, but in spite of resolving to leave matters alone, noticed that a piece had been neatly folded and torn from the top of the earlier letter. The address? 'The vital information,' he breathed. 'Why?'

The next moment Cannon was on his feet, heart pounding, as a voice by his side queried: 'John?'

He had neither heard nor seen Liz come into the kitchen, though she stood almost at his elbow, with a forefinger raised as if she wanted him to listen, or had something vital she needed to tell him. Instead her gaze fell on the papers spread on the table.

'What are you doing? Have you opened Archie's envelope?' she demanded her eyes going to the dresser.

'No . . . I haven't, I — '

'Listen,' she said urgently, 'there's something going on outside. I woke, wondered where you were, then saw lights, there's activity over towards the marsh. It must be the police . . . ' She moved to the back door, adding 'put out the light.'

Cannon followed her outside. The earth had moved on, the moon was lower to the west and the sky was lightening. Even so they could make out lights, a concentration of car

32

headlights, along the road, seawards, past the incident tent, and other lights, torches on the marsh nearer the sea. Another police car streamed its lights and screamed its siren across the fenland. 'The baying of the modern blood-hound,' Cannon muttered and shivered in the autumn pre-dawn.

'Do you think they are looking for Stefan?' Liz asked.

'Yes,' he replied, 'and all of them will be in trouble if they wander about out there.' He slipped an arm around her waist and steered her back inside.

He quickly told her what had happened in the loft and showed her the jacket. 'They probably had a man on watch, or police cars making regular checks at the murder site. I guess they saw him running away.'

'You read these,' he indicated the papers on the table, 'while I — ' he paused to reach for Archie Burns's envelope.

'John, don't . . . ' she began, but he was already pulling the contents from the torn envelope. She shook her head, then slowly sat down as the letters and the translations caught her attention.

'Both men came from a private London employment agency,' John exclaimed, 'how likely is that!'

'And how likely is it that Stefan would be

33

involved in murdering the one man who seems to have been helping him,' Liz said lowering the letters to the table. 'I — ' she broke off, stared wide-eyed at her partner, as the unmistakeable sound of shots came from far across the marshland.

3

It had been six o'clock and nearly full light when all activity ceased and the last police car left the lanes leading to the sea. And to Cannon's relief, it was later Sergeant Maddern who arrived in answer to the call about the envelope left by Archie Burns.

'We've made an arrest,' Sergeant Maddern said as Cannon admitted him through the back door.

'Stefan?' Cannon queried and saw again the figure running frantically away across the fields. The Sergeant accepted Cannon's gesture to a chair and put his cap on the table.

'I wouldn't have thought he was the kind of man to have a gun,' Liz said, dropping teabags into mugs. 'We heard the shots.'

'Shooting at the police won't have helped his case,' Cannon added.

'I'm not even sure the shots were aimed at us,' Maddern said. 'I'm sure it wasn't Hoskins, but that's who the inspector has in custody.'

'Hoskins!' Cannon gasped, then hooted with ironic laughter. 'Hoskins! He wouldn't shoot at anybody! He'd be out there waiting for dawn and the geese flying in from Russia or somewhere.' Cannon, who had picked up the jacket as if to also give this to the sergeant, now hung it on the back of the door.

Liz caught and held his eye for a moment, querying his action, and saw his face take on that inscrutable expression it did not do to question — not immediately at any rate.

'That was automatic fire we heard — a high-powered rifle, or handgun, I would have said.' Cannon slapped his hand on top of the new envelope containing the men's details he had just given the Sergeant, as if he also meant to reclaim that. 'There were enough of you out there to know!'

'Yes,' the sergeant nodded his thanks for the mug of tea and stirred in a large spoonful of sugar, 'but the inspector found a man on the scene with a gun that had just been fired in his hand, and even though it was a double-barrelled twelve bore, and we tried to tell the inspector who Hoskins was, he took him in.'

Cannon frowned, a twelve-bore was not a gun to bring down geese, as both men knew. They also knew Hoskins had other guns, with silencers, and at least one capable of being dismantled for easy concealment under a coat. He was a rogue the local law rather turned a blind eye to — until now. His wonderful memory and local knowledge had been invaluable to the police more than once. Hoskins's long-standing and continuing offence was he ignored the private shooting and fishing rights of the wealthy and made up his pension by poaching. He never, as he said, 'killed anything that wasn't going to grace someone's table,' usually adding if challenged, 'and my prices would shame Robin Hood.' In the bar such remarks either ended the conversation, or resulted in more orders whispered into Hoskins's ear.

'So what was the old devil up to?' Cannon wondered.

'It'll be something to do with his poaching,' Sgt Maddern stated, 'and if luck's with the old boy that particular gun will be one listed on his licence.'

'Did you tell that new inspector, the old boy's always on the marshes, day and night?' Cannon asked.

'You can't tell that man much at all,' Maddern said, then added with the first touch of rancour in his voice, 'told me he's not interested in Fen folklore.'

Liz glanced quickly at this affable sergeant. What a hurtful remark to a man whose family went back generations in that area. She looked from him to her partner, he had just the same inscrutable expression as the sergeant, both masking their real thoughts.

The sergeant sighed, drained his mug, then rose reluctantly and took up his cap. 'Back to HQ,' he said, 'thanks for the tea, Liz.'

'So?' she questioned as the sergeant's car drove away. 'The jacket?'

'Yes,' John said.

'And Stefan running away across the fields?'

'Well, they saw him, chased him, and finished up arresting Hoskins. No,' he paused to take the jacket from the back of the door, drape it over his arm and pick up the jeep keys, 'I found this in the loft this morning, and didn't think to give it to Sergeant Maddern when he came.'

'Spinning a yarn,' Liz said, 'for what reason?'

'Because I can go to the station, find out why they are still holding Hoskins, convince them they shouldn't be, and hopefully bring him home with me.'

'John,' she appealed, not putting into words all he was well aware of: it wasn't their job, they were finished with the police service. The trouble was she also knew her man could not divorce himself from his sense of fairness and an overwhelming need to see justice done.

'And it's the letters,' Cannon went on, 'those translations 'For Nick',' He paused, hand on the door latch, reminding Liz of the

38

way he had often stood stock-still in the middle of a busy Met headquarters, as some aspect of a case struck him. 'I mean why go to that much trouble? A literal translation, why was that so important for a fellow brickie?'

'John, mind what you say at the station, don't make things worse for Hoskins — or for Sergeant Maddern.'

'You should know me better than that.' He gave a humph of laughter. 'I'll even offer to stand bail for the old — '

'He surely won't have been charged!'

'I wouldn't have thought so, though they might impose police bail if they want him back.'

'There's one thing I keep thinking of, that makes me uneasy,' Liz admitted. 'Before we heard what were certainly shots from an automatic weapon, the first two shots I heard were louder, more diffuse — more like a shotgun — but not from the same shotgun. How many people were out there with guns? And didn't it seem as if one lot of shots provoked the other?'

'*Three* guns out there?' Cannon was surprised and shocked by the idea, here in their quiet countryside, but he trusted both Liz's hearing and judgment: that the shots were unconnected, did seem unlikely to him. He was not a great believer in coincidences, and the automatic fire had been so rapid, it had held a sense of spiteful intent. He was anxious to talk to Hoskins, the old man had a keen instinct for such things. 'You'll manage, love, until I get back.'

'Had that been a question I might have answered it,' she told him, sweeping her long hair up and in a swinging fair curtain before tying it into a ponytail.

'You,' he said, 'are acting in a manner likely to cause a disturbance of my peace.'

'Go get Hoskins,' she told him.

'I'll do my very best.'

'Tactfully,' she called after him.

The drive to Boston only took half the time it did in the summer months, when holidaymakers crowded the roads. Though when Cannon reached the police station, all his rehearsed arguments about Hoskins being a man employed by local farmers to keep vermin down (he had once been so employed by a landowner new to the area, much to everyone's amusement), were unneeded as he was informed that Hoskins had been released on police bail some half hour before.

'How was he supposed to get home?' he asked. 'He's an old man.'

'He had money in his pocket,' the constable who looked too young to have left school replied, 'and asked about buses.'

The bus station was in a busy part of town not far from the railway station. Cannon cruised the area, then parked and walked along the bus stands, when suddenly a voice said, 'Looking for me?'

Hoskins was leaning by the side of one of the many stands. Cannon was shocked; not only did his usual wonderful outdoor complexion look drained, his clothes, never more than just respectable, looked crumpled in a different more distressed way. 'I've got the jeep,' Cannon said, 'I'll fetch it. Wait at the end of the road,' he pointed at the exit to the bus station. 'I'll be about five minutes.'

He hurried wondering what kind of questioning and procedures Jones had put Hoskins through. He was even more concerned when Hoskins was beside him in the jeep, for he sat silent, hands screwed tight together between his knees.

'Put you through the mill?' Cannon asked.

'Tried to grind me small: fingerprints, oral swabs, impressions of my boots, photos . . .' He was silent for a moment or two then added, 'He's kept my old twelve-bore and wants my gun licence.'

'You should always carry it when you're out with a gun,' Cannon heard himself say.

'Tell you what, boy, that Yorkshireman's going to do his best to take my licence away for good,' Hoskins concluded. 'Then what'll I do?'

Cannon had to correct his line on the road as he too wondered what on earth Hoskins would do without a gun, it would change — ruin — his life.

'We'll have to think about this,' Cannon said, knowing there were solicitors who specialized in gun licence cases, but what such a solicitor would make of Hoskins' case he was not sure. 'Hopefully it won't happen,' he added, 'meantime I'm taking you to The Trap for some lunch.'

'No,' Hoskins immediately vetoed the idea. 'If you want to help you can listen to what I have to say and then take me back to where I was picked up last night.'

Cannon swung into the next lay-by on the dual carriageway, pulled on the handbrake and switched off the engine.

'What do you know?' Hoskins asked.

Cannon told of Sergeant Maddern's visit.

'He's right,' Hoskins said briefly, 'but I didn't go out to shoot geese . . . '

'No,' Cannon agreed, 'I wondered why a twelve bore?'

'I'm having trouble with someone on one of my best patches, just when the geese'll be flying in,' Hoskins said.

The thought of one poacher resenting

another might have struck Cannon as funny at any other time.

'This man is trigger happy,' Hoskins was saying, 'he'll be shooting the birds as soon as they arrive. I like to give 'em time to rest and feed up. He's been about quite a lot, shot a few rabbits and ducks — often doesn't even bother to check, or pick up, what he's shot. I wanted to give him a scare. I waited for him last night, and when he arrived gave him a barrel up in the air above his head. He reacted by shooting off his own gun — and then there was all this other shooting. The tide was turning and the waves high, but I could hear other movements, other people.'

'You're sure?' Cannon asked, noting that Liz had been right about the three guns.

He nodded. 'I don't know what's going on, but shots like that — they were meant for someone. Then it became like Piccadilly Circus. I heard someone else running fast through the pine needles, though I never saw him, then the police came!' he exclaimed,

Cannon was tempted to say a man couldn't have a quiet poach these days, but did not speak, knowing one often learned far more by just being quiet at the right time.

'I reckon it'll be tied up with that young Nick,' Hoskins said. 'He found something out, and he's been silenced, poor old boy.' He paused, then went on wistfully, 'Just when he had all his life in front of him. Chalk and cheese, the two of them, but good buddies. I tried to find out how they met, but neither of them wanted to answer that question, and like I said, I doubt either of them was really in the building trade before they came here. Did you ever notice Nick's hands, blistered up they were, and getting worse by the day. He'd never been a labourer.'

'I had noticed. He tried wearing gloves,' Cannon said, 'told me he'd been laid off for a time.'

'No,' Hoskins shook his head, 'your hands never go that soft once you've done hard work. Stefan, now, he had seen a bit of manual labour.'

Cannon wondered if he should tell Hoskins about the letters, but felt the old man had enough on his mind for the moment. He reached forward and switched on the engine.

'We won't go the St Andrew's Road,' Hoskins said, 'we'll go along as far as Reed St Thomas, through the village past the church, then up the road to the beach. We'll walk from there.'

They drove past the tall cobbled tower of Reed St Thomas, on to the road to the beach which became increasingly sandy as they passed the basic concrete public lavatories, the closed beach shop and café and into the deserted carpark behind the dunes.

'So what are we looking for?' he asked.

'I have an idea how this man gets on to my patch,' Hoskins said. 'He's not local, he's been around much too long to be a holidaymaker, and I've seen him nowhere else, so I reckon . . . ' Hoskins set off in the steady stride of a man used to covering long distances. He was also remarkably steady on his feet even over the sudden softness of sand between hard clumps of marram grass. Cannon thought Hoskins's ankles were probably stronger than his own from such regular exercise; joggers, he thought, tended to use paths and roads, and the old boy's balance was certainly better than his.

Hoskins was some yards ahead of Cannon, who was pulling his feet from a covering of loose sand, when he exclaimed as if he had found Shangri-La:

'I knew it!' he was pointing ahead, and Cannon not looking where he was going fell down into the stream of sand his own clumsy movements had caused. When he looked up, he saw that Hoskins's excitement was about a small boat, powered by an outboard engine.

Cannon reached his side as Hoskins was examining the boat. 'I thought I heard an outboard motor once before when he was

45

about, but wasn't sure until now,' he said. 'He'd come in at full tide, pull his boat up a little, but . . . ' he paused and looked at Cannon, 'he never went home last night.'

Cannon leaned on the side of the wooden, clinker-built boat, the boat itself was empty, but the powerful four-stroke Suzuki engine looked new. It would be the kind fairly easily to carry — probably cost about a thousand pounds — certainly not a engine you would leave about on a boat all night. So was someone still out here, or had the police picked someone else up? Cannon mentally reviewed the mien of the young constable at the police headquarters in Boston, and shook his head. 'We'd better take a look round,' he said.

They had not walked far. Hoskins was on the shoreline and Cannon nearer the dunes, when Hoskins called him, beckoning urgently. 'The tide's coming in again, it'll be over this in a few minutes,' Hoskins pointed to where in the wet sand there was a confusion of footprints — men's footprints.

'And something's been dragged,' Cannon said pointing to a deeper line scored in the middle of two sets of prints, with the third set of another man standing alongside.

'Or somebody,' Hoskins said as the next wave sent them stepping rapidly back, and they watched a little more of the imprints washing away. 'The man I scared off, taken away in another boat,' he suggested.

The tracks all ended here, so seawards was the only answer. Unless the police had picked him up in a launch, it seemed to give them more questions than answers. Who else was after Hoskins's poacher? Cannon looked inland, taking careful note of where this second boat had come to shore.

'They'll soon all be gone,' Hoskins said as once more they had to step back to avoid the incoming tide, which swept in very rapidly over these wide flat beaches.

'We might find some sign higher up the beach, something to suggest where they came from,' Cannon said.

They walked on, scanning the sands until they reached a tiny peninsula on which grew a mass of fir trees. Here the sand was much disturbed; there were many indentations which could have been made by men's feet, though the soft sand had fallen down into them obscuring any clear outlines. However, they could still make out the straight line made by the object, or the person, who had been dragged. If it was a man, Cannon felt he must be a heavy man — the scored line was deep — but Stefan, he thought, was quite a slight man.

They were just at the edge of the firs when Hoskins stopped, a swirl of flies coming up from near his feet. He peered down, then beckoned Cannon, as he very delicately stirred the sandy soil. It was darker than anywhere around, and even as they stood there the disturbed flies returned.

Cannon was reminded of a lecture he had attended early in his police training, when students were told that the earliest example of forensic science was from ancient China. An important man had been murdered by soldiers. The officer ordered his men out into the sunshine, where they were made to stand to attention with their long-handled spears in the air. The two men, whose weapons attracted the flies to the traces of blood left on their weapons, were summarily executed.

Hoskins stood, head raised, feeling the wind. 'Yes,' he said, 'the wind was from the south east last night. This is where the shots came from. This is where someone was shot.'

Assassinated, was the word that came to Cannon's mind. They had seen no sign of blood, or flies, anywhere else. Dead men don't bleed.

4

Cannon decided it was he who would tell inspector Jones what they had found, leaving Hoskins well out of the picture.

Before dusk that evening it involved him in another walk with the inspector, first to where Hoskins had found the blooded sand. Although there was nothing now to be seen, no flies, and heavy rain showers had eliminated anything visible to the naked eye, CSI were again summoned, and they took away deep samples of sand from the spot.

Cannon, being very careful not to slip into the plural 'we', detailed where the footprints and the line between two of sets of prints had indicated that something, or someone, had been dragged to the edge of the sea and he believed taken off by boat. But since that time others had walked there with children and dogs and there was, again, little to see. He sensed the inspector's growing scepticism.

'What were you doing here,' the inspector swept his arm across the deserted stretch of shore as another onslaught of rain swept in from the sea, 'on this particular beach?'

'I walk a lot,' he replied.

'On *this* particular beach?' Jones repeated, 'at *this* particular time?'

'It's a good place to see the over-wintering geese fly in,' he said, having gathered that much from Hoskins.

'You keep cropping up,' Jones accused, stepping across his path.

'I live here,' he answered, holding the man's gaze through the slanting curtain of rain.

Jones grunted. 'Is there owt else you want me to see in this godforsaken place, or can we get inside somewhere?' the inspector asked.

'There was a boat pulled up on the beach a little further on,' Cannon said, 'you might want to have a look at it.'

'Why should you think that?'

Cannon was aware that his own waterproof trousers and top were far more efficient than Jones's mac and woolly hat. 'It might give a clue to who else was around at the time,' he shouted above the pounding rain. 'You took Hoskins in, but I'd stake my life that he had nothing to do with any of it.'

Jones leant towards him to shout back, 'Fortunately for you, these days it'd only be your freedom, not your life, you'd be staking.'

In the middle of his sentence the rain ceased as suddenly as it had begun.

'The other thing,' Cannon said, ignoring

the implications of that last remark, 'there was an expensive outboard motor, not the sort of thing to leave lying around . . . but . . . ' He stopped walking, and heard Jones's exasperated grunt behind him.

'Don't tell me,' he said, 'it's gone,' then he added scathingly, 'so another wild goose chase then.'

Cannon felt scored against, but did not bother to answer as he wondered, if Hoskins' poacher had retrieved his boat, who had been shot and dragged away? Whose blood would forensics find in the sand? Stefan's? He recalled the desperate figure running from his hayloft.

'Let's get back,' Jones said pulling off his soaked woolly hat and wringing it out. 'I've enough hard evidence to keep me busy, without chasing . . . missing boats.'

'Stefan?' The name was immediately on Cannon's lips.

Jones stared and sucked his teeth. 'I'll drop my hand on the right man's shoulder, don't you fret.' He turned and began to walk back, Cannon with his own jeep in the beach carpark did not bother to catch him up.

When Billy Brompton was his first customer that evening, Cannon was to learn just what Jones had meant. Billy, a powerful man, who drove and now owned his own lorry was a regular for breakfasts, and often returned to the pub in the evenings still in his navy work overalls. Tonight he was dressed-up — black leather jacket, blue shirt, best jeans — and carried a small holdall.

'Going away?' Cannon asked as he pulled the man's usual pint of bitter.

'Only because I have to,' he growled hoisting his impressive weight on to a bar stool.

'Not bad news, I hope,' Cannon said studying the man's face.

'Been under the wife's feet all day, that's always bad news.'

'No delivery today?'

'No lorry,' Billy thumped the side of his clenched fist on the counter. 'Went to load, and no bloody lorry. Reported it to the police — they've found it — but it's at bloody Newhaven! I've got to fetch it, but I can't have it back until the forensic people 'ave finished with it. You should hear the wife! She ain't best pleased, I can tell you, apart from the loss of earnings. I mean I love 'er to bits, but when she gets going . . . '

Cannon grinned, and put a foaming pint in front of Billy. The lorry-driver's stormy relationship with the mercurial and often violent Madge was a regular source of amusement in the bar, when Billy came in quite often displaying an injury from the latest skirmish.

'They think illegals pinched the lorry,' he said blowing out his lips in disbelief, adding, 'I thought they all wanted to come into the country, not escape.'

So what Jones thought was his 'hard evidence' must be that Stefan had stolen the lorry to leave the area, and the country. Cannon was convinced he would do no such thing, he was sure there was no way Stefan would return home without his sister. She was his reason for being here. The mystery was the tie up with Nick's murder . . . but if Jones was concentrating on Stefan being out of the area, it gave Cannon an idea — something he could do.

'But why the clothes and the holdall?' Cannon asked.

'I've a mate who's going to pick me up from here and run me down south, he's got to do the Newhaven — Dieppe crossing. I'm going to stop down there until the police release my lorry. I might even get a load to come back this way with a bit of luck. Chap I'm going with has some contacts.'

After they had closed their doors that night Cannon sat, thoughtful, in the kitchen as Liz made their usual last thing cup of tea. It was a time when they wound down from the buzz of activity and customers, chatted about things they had been told or overheard during the evening. But tonight Cannon was quiet, sipping his drink.

'So Billy has gone to Newhaven?' she prompted, watching him carefully.

'Hmm, didn't know the man who came to pick him up.'

'From just north of Boston he said,' Liz replied.

'I'm going to have a run into Boston tomorrow,' Cannon said.

'Why?'

'I'm going to drop in at that pub where all the immigrant workers gather. I thought I might learn something.'

'John!' She tutted her disapproval.

'I have to,' he said, 'Jones is on the wrong track, and I'm beginning to feel if I don't find some answers he's going to haul Hoskins in again — or me.'

'You?' Liz exclaimed.

'Apparently I keep 'cropping up', first jogging, then walking, I suppose he means. Jones doesn't understand the area, what goes on, he doesn't listen! He doesn't even have the right clothes.'

'That's a bit petty,' she remarked, then reminisced, 'first discipline for good policing, I was told: Listen and learn, watch and wait.'

'So I'll go in the morning, have a lunchtime pint, do a bit of listening and learning.'

'And stick out like a sore thumb,' she said. 'No one is going to come and talk to you voluntarily, not to a stranger in a place like that.'

'Then I'll just watch and wait,' he said grinning at her, but he had a question he intended to ask in that bar, an inquiry he hoped would bring some comeback.

★　★　★

The aptly named Stump's Shadow public house might well, Cannon calculated as he walked towards it, literally have been in the shadow of St Botolph's tower if the sun had been out. At eighty-three metres high and universally know as Boston Stump, the church was visible from the far side of The Wash, and had dominated the Fenland landscape for over seven hundred years.

Cannon smiled as he pushed through into the pub's foyer, the multi-language problem was solved by the five doors off it *all* having pictures of what lay beyond: the usual signs for male and female toilets; a depiction of a counter with a man leaning on it; a table with a glass and chips in a basket, and finally a table with a cloth and formal place settings.

From this last room an extra buzz of noise and enjoyment came, and as Cannon stood there this door opened and a man and woman came out laughing and flushed. He caught a glimpse of a wedding party, a large cake on a table, girls and women in dresses with many ribbons, but the meal and ceremony must have been over, for while the girls and women stood clapping in time to guitars and a zither, the men were dancing in a circle, arms over each others' shoulders, heads down, singing, stamping to a rhythm they all knew. Cannon smiled and nodded to those in the doorway, they beckoned him in, but he held up his hands in regret that he could not join them, but wishing to make some gesture he kissed his hand and blew the kiss in the direction of the bride.

Pushing the door depicting the counter, he saw a crowded bar, and caught the tailend of a conversation in English.

'So what do you think has happened to Ivo?'

'Said too much, and pushed his privileges too far,' was the other man's verdict.

Cannon paused in the doorway as he heard the same name Stefan's sister had mentioned in her letter: 'I met a chap, Ivo, in a pub in Boston.' Then he was reminded of Liz's prediction, as eyes turned to him as he stepped right into the room and conversations, in several languages, ceased.

In the time it took him to walk from door to counter the atmosphere changed. The whole bar became alerted to his presence as though someone had cried, 'I spy strangers'. Some who could not see him properly moved forward, peered, shrugged their mystification and dropped back. But one man in particular came forward and stayed at the corner of the bar so he could look directly at Cannon.

Not over tall, but large, powerful, swarthy, his suit was tailored, his broad fingers sported several impressive gold rings, a diamond star flashed from one as he spread his hands before him on the counter.

Portuguese, Cannon guessed, and from his sardonic manner the man felt invincible. He had met the type before, in illegal gambling dens, race tracks and casinos, anywhere where big money was made and spent. A man who had most likely stepped outside the law to make his fortune. He oozed self-importance, this was his world and he was king.

Cannon ordered lager from the barman. When he had paid, he looked up again to find the man's gaze still fixed on him.

Cannon held his stare, then deliberately and loudly cleared his throat to ask, 'Do you know of anyone here who will do some translating for a Croatian friend of mine.'

Cannon felt interest flutter in some corners of the bar, but the big man grunted with laughter as if amused by the audacity of this newcomer. Then, as if he too sensed interest, he slapped his hands hard on the counter as if calling all to order. He shook his head meaningfully at Cannon, then slowly glanced all around the bar. Those who did not drop or shake their heads sat rigid, motionless. Repression and fear pervaded that room.

Cannon sipped his pint, then added to the bar at large, 'My friend will pay well for good translations.' His words caused a kind of mini-stir and he added 'real good money'. It was what all these immigrants had come over here to earn, but the big man laughed louder, and again any tide of interest retreated.

He considered a confrontation, but decided he would gain nothing but trouble for himself and these hard-working people. So he merely took his time over his drink and looked around, pulled a newspaper towards himself, saw it was Polish, but looked at the pictures anyway. He was halfway down his drink before conversations began again, hesitantly, quietly, none in English.

At a gesture from the big man the barman poured clear spirit of some kind from a bottle and put glass and bottle on the counter. The

Portuguese undoubtedly intended to stay where he was until Cannon left, and certainly no one was going to approach him however much money he offered. The only other thing he gleaned as he finished his pint was that although the big man was dark and did not at first sight look particularly energetic, his complexion was tanned, suggesting he spent a fair amount of time in the open air, and some of that bulk could be hard muscle.

Putting down his empty glass Cannon nodded his goodbye to the barman who moved his head fractionally, but as he left there was once more a fall in conversation levels. If he had obeyed his instincts he might have run, and he had to consciously stop himself looking round to see if he was being followed.

He definitely felt he was in the shadow of something far more sinister than Boston's Stump as he walked away. In the six years he had been a landlord he'd had many an awkward moment in his own bar, an odd customer or two becoming aggressive, but never had he felt an atmosphere of such general apprehension — fear — as had pervaded the bar of the Stump's Shadow. A chill ran over his flesh and he shuddered. What was the saying, 'someone had walked over your grave'.

He was not far from where he had left his jeep when there was the sound of someone scurrying after him. This time he did turn and as he did a small, slightly-built man in a shabby, black, over-large, overcoat half raised a hand as if to confirm it was Cannon he was trying to catch — then he too looked behind himself, and seeming satisfied, trotted up to come level with Cannon.

'Sir,' he said, 'I can do good translations.' Again he looked back along the street.

'Do you want to come and sit in my vehicle to talk?' Cannon asked.

He nodded. Once he was in the jeep which Cannon had parked in a quiet side-street, the little man seemed to relax a little. 'In Zagreb I was a clerk,' he said. 'I am rarely hired for land work here, but I want to work, I need to earn money — so if you want translations doing, I am your man.'

'Perhaps it is you my friend, Stefan, mentioned,' Cannon said and watched the little Croatian's face brighten.

'Oh yes, Stefan like many, speaks . . . ' he shrugged, 'OK, gets by, but does not translate on paper very good.'

'You did letters for him,' Cannon said keeping his voice flat, neutral, 'from his sister.'

The man nodded but gave Cannon a quick

sideways glance. 'He has found her?'

'No, I am trying to help him — and his friend, Nick.' There was no response. It was clear that if this man had heard of the murder he had no idea there was any connection with Stefan. Cannon went on: 'I need your help, well, Stefan and I both need your help.' Unsure how else to continue, and keep this man interested, Cannon leaned forward, took his wallet from his back pocket and extracted a twenty pound note.

The man looked at it with a kind of hunger. 'I need the work, but . . . I think you are . . . ' He looked at Cannon and then at the old jeep.

'I am a pub landlord,' he stated before the man could begin speculating.

'Who needs Croatian translator? Why has Stefan not come himself? He knows me, knows I would do a good job.' The man's hand was on the doorhandle, suspicion written large across his face.

Cannon was desperate not to lose this contact. 'Will you listen to why I am here and not Stefan?' he asked.

There was hesitation, a glance along the street.

'It will not take long,' Cannon said, waiting for some sign of collaboration, and when his hand fell from the doorhandle, told him everything as precisely as possible.

'Everyone has heard of the murder,' the man said, ' . . . and this was Stefan's friend?'

He nodded. 'Antonija mentioned a man named Ivo, I thought she might have met him in the Stump's Shadow.'

'Yes,' the Croatian said and his hand closed around the twenty pound note. 'I am sure she did, he's usually around some part of every day, but the last two days . . . ?'

'Does he do field work?'

'No, he is lucky man, he works as a security guard, good money, regular hours. No one seems to know where he is, if he is ill . . . He should let Mr de Garro know — he is not a patient man.'

'Mr de Garro?' Cannon queried, 'sounds Portuguese.'

'Yes, you will have seen him in the bar — at the counter.'

'The man with the gold rings?

'Vasco de Garro, a man with many business interests, many to do with us foreign workers. No one dares cross him.'

'What do his business interests include?'

There was a prolonged lifting of the shoulders. 'I think he has interest in the pub.'

'The Stump's Shadow?'

'Yes, and I know he has a Health Hydro, the other side of the estuary somewhere. It is where Ivo works on security. There is also an estate where Mr de Garro arranges shoots for local big wigs. Keeps them sweet, as you say.'

'Does Ivo like hunting?'

Surprised by the question the interpreter nevertheless said, 'Yes, he always says he loves it . . . so does his boss, and they often talk fishing in the bar, but — '

'But?' Cannon prompted.

'Ivo talks *too* much, does not treat Mr de Garro right, not enough respect.' He stopped, looking as if worse thoughts overwhelmed him.

Cannon saw him shudder. It was as if the feeling in the bar was being acted out by this man.

'He takes . . . ' Again a shudder and a troubled glance at Cannon as if for help, 'he takes . . . '

'His life in his hands,' Cannon suggested and the man nodded.

⋆　⋆　⋆

'His name is Alamat,' Cannon told Liz when he returned to The Trap in the middle of the afternoon to find her relaxing for once in their first floor lounge. 'He needs work, but I don't want to put him in any danger. He's memorized our phone number and promised to ring if he has any news of Stefan.'

'And if you need to contact him?' Liz asked.

'At the hostel where he lives,' he answered but remembering how reluctantly this information had been given, felt that Pavao and many of the immigrants lived in a cross between apprehension and bravado. He certainly did not want to make anyone's life more difficult.

'So this Ivo works as a security guard at a Health Hydro,' Liz began.

'I've never heard of such a place anywhere around here.'

'Ah well, perhaps not your scene, but . . . ,' she reached over to the coffee table and pulled the glossy county magazine from the newspapers. 'I'm sure there is one not that far away, there's always an advert in here for it.' She turned the pages then passed it to him. 'There's a little map at the top showing exactly where it is.'

He studied the full page advert, but it was not the picture of the mansion and interior shots showing treatments, pools, people lying in blissful poses on and under towels that caught his eye; it was the bottom quarter of the opposite page, which offered fishing in naturally screened and regularly restocked pools. The map was much the same as the one for the Health Hydro, and more interesting than that, he saw the telephone numbers were the same.

'What have you spotted?' Liz asked knowing the kind of enlightened look that came over her partner's face when an idea struck.

'I'm going fishing,' he said.

5

Cannon was in his garage rooting out his fly fishing tackle when someone darkened the doorway. He turned expecting to see Liz, with another reason for him not to go to the south side of the estuary that afternoon; the last had been the blustery weather. It was almost as if she had conjured up the best reason of all, when he turned to see that it was Inspector Jones who was taking his light.

'Inspector,' he greeted propping up a rod and line he had experimentally assembled.

'Going fishing?' Jones asked.

'My partner thinks it's too rough,' he answered.

'You're out and about quite a bit,' he paused then got down to business. 'Mind telling me why you visited Boston, and in particular the Stump's Shadow yesterday?' Jones sucked his teeth as he waited for an answer.

For a wild moment Cannon wondered if Jones had him under constant surveillance, but knew it was more likely that a fairly regular police eye was kept on possible hotspots. The Stump's Shadow was quite often the target for attacks by local youths, usually the worse for drink, and occasional rough retaliation from the immigrants. A range of answers, true and false, flashed through his mind, in the end he just said, 'Curiosity,' hoping he had only been seen going into the pub — not overheard inside.

'About?' Jones snapped back.

'Immigrants in general, I suppose.'

'And in particular?' Jones took half a step nearer to him, reached over and took up the assembled rod and line.

Cannon resented the action. 'No one in particular,' he answered, and as he went to take the rod from the inspector, Jones moved it out of his reach. Cannon knew he would have found this man objectionable in whatever sphere of life he had encountered him. It was what Liz called a tribal hate left over from the primordeal forest.

'So you were not looking for Stefan Tomac?'

'My builder? I didn't know his surname,' Cannon said.

'An illegal immigrant,' Jones said.

'He must have had bloody good papers,' Cannon stated. 'Archie Burns would not have employed anyone who had dodgy looking documents. So, if he was illegal, who helped him? Nick? If he did he seems to have paid with his life.'

'So another brickie got him top class papers,' Jones laughed, but Cannon remembered the translations headed 'For Nick' and was about to say more when there was the sound of foot-steps and voices coming out to the garage. This time it was Liz — with the CSI officer, Franklyn.

'I want CSI to go over your hayloft, do you have a problem with that?' Jones snapped.

'Not at all,' Cannon said greeting Franklyn. 'Stefan was almost certainly up there, it was where I found the jacket.'

'And read the contents of the pockets,' Jones stated.

'Yes, I did, to be sure whose coat it was,' Cannon replied.

'Going fishing?' Franklyn asked the Inspector, who did not answer. Franklyn laughed adding, 'I'll get on shall I?'

Liz offered to show him the trapdoor up into the loft, also where the ladder was kept, adding to John, 'If you and the Inspector are busy talking . . . '

'Oh! I think we've finished for now,' Jones said, but waiting until the other two had turned away, he thrust the fishing-rod towards Cannon and hissed, 'Stop meddling or I'll reel you in.'

Cannon repressed all he really wanted to say, but did ask, 'Have they released Billy

Brompton's lorry yet?' The look of pure hatred Jones gave him, convinced Cannon that he was right, there had been little point in chasing after Billy's lorry. He knew his gut feeling about Stefan was right too: he would never return home without his sister — or without knowing her fate.

* * *

By the time Jones and CSI had gone, so also had the best of the afternoon. In their first floor sitting-room Liz covertly watched her partner as she looked through a watercolour painting magazine — a hobby she intended to take up. John had finally been convinced by the shortness of daylight and the rising Easterly that fishing anywhere was not an option for that day.

She raised her eyebrows as he went to his telescope, pushing it to its fullest extent to the north before sitting down and slowly, slowly, bringing it across its complete range of coast — the land, thick reed-beds and seashore. She knew the sea would be spectacular now as it was being driven in by a high wind on the rising tide.

To be able to view the strength and majesty of such awesome seas without having to be out and about always felt to Liz a very special privilege, but she knew John would be silently fretting about his lost afternoon. She, on the other hand, was very content he had been delayed, even by Inspector Jones. She was pleased he was inside, safe, secure, under her eye — but then she slowly lowered the magazine. John had stopped his leisurely scan and was concentrating on one spot, his right hand going forward to adjust the lenses.

She found herself swallowing apprehensively as she watched his posture change from relaxed observation to intense concentration. 'What is it?' she asked, 'what have you seen?'

'I'm not sure . . . ' he began, then, seeming to screw his eye more firmly to the telescope, he said, 'Yes, I am sure — but don't believe it.' He swung round to face her.

'John?'

'It's Hoskins,' he said as he rose, repeating, 'I'm sure its Hoskins!' as he reached and flung open the door of their cosy sittingroom. 'He's out there — on that beach. I have to go . . . '

'Why, would . . . ' she shook her head, then jumped up, called down the stairs after him. 'Wait, I'm coming.'

'You stay there,' he called back.

She grabbed a coat and shoved her feet into her walking boots — heard wheels screech as his jeep swept out of the garage. She paused long enough to key in the burglar alarm, lock the door, then ran to her own classic MG.

She knew the track he would take, rough, narrow, but the nearest way to the beach he could see through the telescope. It would do her MG no good at all. In minutes she was parked behind the jeep. She closed her door, and the jeep's, and ran. By the time she reached the top of the sandy incline, John was at the sea's edge. Beyond him she saw Hoskins, in the water, waves at waist height one moment, over his shoulders the next.

What was the old man doing? Had he gone mad? Was he trying to drown himself? He looked likely to succeed. Then her heart lurched as she knew whatever it cost him, John would never let that happen.

With the wind straight in her face, she had to keep her head well tucked down even to breathe. Then, as another dark shape appeared beyond Hoskins, she saw exactly what he was doing — or trying to do.

There was someone else in the water, a man, one arm waving wildly, desperately. 'He'll never get to him,' was her thought, but then she saw John already deep in the sea, shoulders working, arms flailing, as he fought his way towards them. One moment she could see all three men, the next no one, as a huge wave reared to a tremendous height. She saw Hoskins duck, as if to go beneath the wall of water. Her thoughts as chaotic as the sea, she wondered if it was a seventh roller, or was that a myth, but when it fell with a thundering crash, she felt the spray from it soaking her face, tasted the salt in her mouth. She forced herself to stand still, knowing if she ran down the slope she would not see so well — so there for long, long, seconds she waited . . .

It was Hoskins who rose like a dark streaming spectre from the green and white water. He was in the trough of the breaking roller, but still going forward, deeper, fighting against the tide. The dark shape of the waving man was some fifteen metres away from him.

But where was John? She peered, searched desperately, then a movement to her left, much further off than she could have imagined, caught her eye, and she saw him. He must have been caught in the upsurge and now sprawled in the shallows as if spit from a gigantic spin dryer.

'John!' she shouted as she ran towards him, though the wind made her voice a whisper. She saw him struggling up, and before he rose from his knees to his feet he was on his way back in to help Hoskins.

Oh, God! Then it became prayer: God, help them all. Her mind raced as fast and unruly as the tide. 'All . . . For those in peril on the sea' . . . And Hoskins . . . Hoskins must be near the other man . . .

Much taller, younger, stronger, John was making better progress, swimming hard. He was near as the next outsized roller lifted the drowning man and drove him down full on to Hoskins, and once more all three disappeared under a towering wall of water.

Liz was thigh-deep before she saw them again, surfacing en masse, as if welded together; John bear-hugging Hoskins, while Hoskins seemed to have the man he had gone in to save by the scruff of his neck.

She reached them, went to Hoskins's other side, and between them they reached the shallows. 'Hold the body,' John shouted to her.

The body? She turned to look down at the man Hoskins was dragging in by the collar; the coat had ridden up obscuring the face. The arm that had seemed to beckon so urgently floated and flopped freely even in shallow water. It must have been broken in several places — shattered — there was no other movement. John was right: it was a body.

She had to squeeze Hoskins's waist hard and shout in his ear, 'It's alright, Alan, I've got him,' before he let go and John could support their best customer beyond the reach of the waves.

In moments John was back by her side and taking the man under his armpits, hauling him up near to where Hoskins sat. The face was now revealed and Liz saw this man had all the pallor of one who had been in the water many, many hours. Hoskins staggered to her side.

'It's the man who poached my best places,' he turned to tell them, and he did not need to remind Cannon of the shooting they had all heard.

John stooped and lifted the bottom of the zipped black leather jacket coat which was holed in several places. The light jersey underneath had its own tidemark where blood had been soaked and rinsed by the sea — higher on the chest the stains were deeper, redder.

John and Hoskins exchanged glances. 'We'll get you indoors,' John said nodding down to the murdered man. 'He's not going anywhere . . . '

★ ★ ★

Liz found dry warm underclothes and a tracksuit that would fit Hoskins, then the

74

same for John, bundling them in through the bathroom door along with more warm towels. She then stripped off in the bedroom. By the time the two men were dressed she had tea waiting for them in the kitchen.

They sat in silence for a moment or two, hands curled around the hot mugs, sipping, listening to the wind howling around the pub, as if complaining of the building's very presence, daring to impede its path.

'I should have known he was dead,' Hoskins reflected. 'A high tide always brings its flotsam in at that spot.'

John reached down a bottle from the kitchen dresser and poured a little brandy into each mug. 'I'll report it to the police,' he told Hoskins. 'We don't want you hauled in for questioning again.' He paused, then asked, 'So what *were* you doing out there?'

Liz resisted the temptation to say it was probably because he had no woman at home to persuade him to stay in when the weather was so awful.

'I have orders to fulfil,' Hoskins said, a touch of indignation in his voice, 'but then I saw that old boy in the sea, I thought he was . . . well, that he needed help.' He paused then added, 'and I've left my shotgun in the dunes — and my bike.' He made as if to rise.

'You sit still,' Cannon told him.

'We should have thought,' Liz said, 'well, about the bike.' Hoskins cycled everywhere.

'And the gun,' Cannon added. 'I'll go fetch them in the jeep. Tell me roughly whereabouts.'

'My bike, on the left of the main pullover to the beach, my gun . . . well, I just stuck her upright in the sand when I went into the water — in a line with where my old bike is, I'd say.'

'I'll go at once,' Cannon said. 'The longer we delay ringing the police — '

'The more likely the inspector is to find out we've not been telling the whole truth,' Liz said, thinking John would cover up for Hoskins, but by doing so put himself firmly in Jones's sights yet *again*.

She followed him to the door, handing him his waxed jacket and their most powerful torch. 'I'll ring the police as soon as we've got him home,' he told her, then stooped to kiss her cheek.

It made her feel worse, made her realize he knew *exactly* how serious their situation could become.

He heard Hoskins apologize to Liz as she went back inside.

'I forgot all about 'em . . . '

Then the door closed and he had a strange, but strong, sense of being excluded from his own life. He crouched defensively as the wind hit him once more, then pulled on the jacket as he ran to the jeep.

He drove without headlights. There was just enough daylight to see, though he guessed lighting up time was well past. He needed his eyes well adjusted to the gloom before he started searching for a gun stuck upright in the sand.

The jeep lurched violently into an unseen rut. He swore, fought for control, wondered what the hell he was getting into — then remembered the defeated looking Hoskins he had found in the Boston bus station. There was no way he was going to let the old rogue be taken in and cross-questioned again.

To his relief he located the bike easily. He stooped to lift it and saw there was something beneath the handlebars, a dark mass. He put out an exploratory hand. 'Hell!' he exclaimed as he touched something soft, yielding and vaguely warm. He tried again more gingerly, tutted, and lifted a couple of rabbits already gutted and strung together by their hind legs. Not only was he retrieving bike and gun, but Hoskins's stock-in-trade. He slung the rabbits over one shoulder and balanced the bike by its crossbar on his other, carried them to his jeep and loaded them in the back.

The gun was not going to be so easy. The

fast darkening horizon promised a rain squall, but he did not want to use the torch. In this landscape where street lights and passing cars were well inland, and the nearest lighthouse miles away, a solitary traveller might well be alerted by a sudden beam of light.

He had taken a line straight down the beach from where the bike had been, but found nothing. Now he tacked backwards and forwards, gradually approaching the body.

He paused by the man's side, then knelt and shrouding the torch with his coat, clicking it on to study the man's face. The face could hardly have been said to indicate the man was at peace, a marble effigy of surprise and agony might be nearer, but that he was of Eastern European origin there was no doubt. He also wondered if, as well as being the man who poached Hoskins's patches, he was not also the missing Ivo, the man Stefan's sister had met in the Boston pub, the man who had been missing from his usual haunts for a day or two, and the man the translator had said was as keen on hunting as his Portuguese boss?

An important link in some kind of chain, Cannon thought, and though his fingers itched to go through the man's pockets he resisted the temptation. An interference too far even for him.

As he knelt there the wind was driving the black clouds nearly overhead. If he was going to find the shotgun, and find it he must, he would have to risk using the torch. He also decided he should pull the body further up the beach; wind-driven tides were notoriously unpredictable — there was little to stop them rushing miles inland once they topped a certain level.

The wind was straight in his face as he walked backwards, hauling the body higher. He stumbled and fell several times and at the third fall he saw, or sensed, a movement to his left, towards where he had found the bike. He abandoned the body, pulled his torch from his pocket and swung the beam that way, just in time to see the red brush of a fox disappearing into the dunes.

He wondered if the smell of the gutted rabbits had attracted it, or, and his own stomach lurched at the thought, was it the body? Foxes, like dogs, have a sense of smell a hundred times greater than that of a human being, another fact he had absorbed during early police training. It could even, he supposed, have trailed Hoskins from where he had gutted the rabbits.

He had switched the torch off when he realized there had been something sticking upright in the sands at the extreme range of the beam. Could it be that simple? He strode over and found the gun, its stock pushed deep into the sand. 'Thanks Mr Fox,' he breathed, brushed the sand off the stock before he broke the barrel. He was mildly surprised to find Hoskins had left it loaded. His haste to help the beckoning man had indeed been urgent.

Back at his jeep he found the fox claiming his own reward, for as he approached, the predator leapt out of the back, head high to lift and carry away the two tied rabbits.

'He'd've had to be hungry to tackle you and the back of that old jalopy,' Hoskins said when told.

Cannon's love of his old Willys jeep was another thing Hoskins pulled his leg about, so he judged the old boy was more or less back on form. Cannon also noted that the brandy bottle had gone down a little more.

'Good enough to take you home in,' he retorted, 'now you're warmed through.'

'Might 'ave got a medal if he'd been alive,' Hoskins reflected.

'Yeah!' Cannon exclaimed, 'and the way you were going you might have got a wreath, come on, you stupid old bugger, let's get you out of the way before I phone Jones. He won't be awarding you anything.'

'You'll keep me out of it?' There was real

anxiety as Hoskins asked.

'Yes,' Cannon confirmed, 'I shall say I found the body at the water's edge, and pulled it up so the tide couldn't take it out to sea again.'

'What about your wet clothes?' Liz asked Hoskins.

'Best I take 'em out of the way, I reckon.'

'Yes,' Cannon agreed with alacrity, seeing Liz wavering, probably wanting to wash, dry and iron the lot. 'Just put them all in a black sack.'

She scowled at him, but as Hoskins nodded at her, she compromised folding them into a large hessian shopping bag.

The drive to Hoskins's cottage took only minutes and once the bike was offloaded and in its usual place under the lean-to, Cannon followed Hoskins inside carrying the bag and gun. Hoskins turned to take them from him.

'Put your heater on,' Cannon nodded to the halogen heater standing in the kitchen, a new addition.

'I'll put a match to my fire in the sitting room.'

'Let's go and do it then,' he said, and when Hoskins still hesitated, added, 'I have to report back to Liz you know.'

'Yes, well then, you're a lucky man,' the old boy said, but instead of leading the way to his sitting room he flipped the switch to the heater. 'I've had years enough looking after myself, I'll be OK. You get off.'

Cannon hesitated, then nodded and for a second they regarded each other in silence, as if both felt there should be something more. Then, hesitantly, Hoskins extended a hand. Cannon took it and they shook, confirming some kind of pact, or some kind of unspoken greater understanding about life and of each other.

It was Liz who opened the bar for the night's trade while John rang the police, and mentally prepared himself for Jones. Twenty minutes later it was Chief Inspector Helen Moore and Sergeant Maddern, in plain clothes, who walked into the near deserted bar.

'Not more trouble,' a mate of Billy Brompton's muttered, as he pulled his darts from the board.

Cannon lifted the counter flap and ushered them through to the kitchen.

'You and Liz are having a very unsettling time,' Chief Inspector Moore said, adding, as both took in Sergeant Maddern in civvies, 'I've detailed Sergeant Maddern to Detective Inspector Jones for the time being.'

Cannon glanced at Maddern's implacable face and wondered if anyone could possibly mistake him for anything other than a policeman in whatever he wore, even his pyjamas — the reason perhaps he had, on a previous occasion, gone from plain clothes back into uniform. He did not envy the man, but thanked whatever lucky star he had up there for sending this man and this knowledgeable but humane woman, recently promoted to chief inspector. He and Liz knew her well. He wondered how Jones coped with her. 'You'll want to go straight to the body,' he said.

They both nodded. 'You can tell us what happened on the way,' Helen Moore said. 'Guess Liz will manage while you're away, on a night like this anyway.'

6

The next morning on his usual early morning jog Cannon found himself drawn in the direction of the same beach, but it was a different world. The sea at low tide lay calm as a drawn blue line beyond what looked like miles and miles of sand, artistically streaked with estuary mud. The only sign there had been a storm was the huge piles of detritus at high water level and the added freshness Cannon always noticed after, what the locals called, 'a good blow'.

Away to his left, inland a little, he could just make out a lazy curl of smoke from Paul's cottage chimney. To his right was the scene of the action the previous night. He would have liked to have done a little beachcombing in that direction, but he was quite sure police presence would have been stepped up at first light. Stupid to be found hanging around again; neither he nor more casual walkers would be welcome and neither, he thought, would the dog which came into sight, rushing full-tilt at a group of gulls busy pecking among the storm debris. Ears flying, the Springer Spaniel put them to flight, the game obviously never to ever let a gull land again. Then the fact that it was a Springer made him watch more closely. There was one person who had such a dog who might legitimately be going to the scene. He waited, saw the dog tear back towards a slim trousered figure, which came into view beyond a breakwater. He knew by the length of her free stride that it was the Chief Inspector exercising her beloved dog, Polly, and no doubt also intending to review where the body had been recovered in daylight.

He was about to turn for home when he realised she had seen him. She raised a hand and changed course. He went to meet her.

'Good morning, John, never know there'd been a bit of a blow.' She swept an arm across the calm canvas.

He called his greeting, and smiled at her use of the local understatement. She had fitted in, always treated local knowledge with respect, probably the reason she had attached Maddern to Jones for this case.

He kicked at a pile of thick net and ropes, then noticed a tangle of nylon line inextricably tangled with a huge swathe of seaweed. 'Far too much of that stuff about,' he commented.

'But not the cause of death this time,' Helen said gently. 'You would have seen the

85

man you dragged in shore had been shot several times.'

'Yes, and most likely the shots from the automatic we heard the night Hoskins was taken in.'

'Little doubt I would say,' she confirmed, and watching him stir the nylon tangle of illegal small-meshed net added, 'too much of that, and two too many murders.'

Cannon sensed a lecture coming.

'John,' and there was censure in the first word, 'I know you, but Inspector Jones is the new boy on the patch, all he sees is this publican who keeps turning up when there's trouble — more than that — John Cannon seems to go seeking it out,' she paused meaningfully. 'Jones will be around later today, but if you found out anything from your visit to the Stump's Shadow you think we should know . . . '

Cannon half turned away and began to walk slowly on; Helen fell into step beside him. Movement gave him time to think, and it was easier to arrange truth with discretion when the person you were talking to was not looking you directly in the eye.

He told of his concern for Stefan Tomac and his belief that Jones was wrong to think he was either guilty of Nick's murder, or that he might have left the country. 'He should

86

concentrate on tracing the good English family who employed Antonija Tomac illegally for little more than her keep, pushing her into worse trouble so she could send money home.'

'Jim Maddern is on that,' she told him. 'Jones is looking into the London employment agency these men came from, but . . . curiouser and curiouser . . . '

'Let me guess,' Cannon interrupted, 'it doesn't exist.'

'Right, so . . . ?'

'So, what are we asking?' Cannon posed the question. 'First, perhaps, how two men presumably from London arrive for jobs which Archie Burns would have only advertised in the local *Eastern Daily Press*.'

She shook her head. 'Easy enough to print convincing letter-heads from an employment agency, for anything come to that. Anyone with a computer can. But, as you say, why?'

'Why?' Cannon echoed. 'We know Stefan came into this country, and Nick was born in London, that I'm sure of, but he's far more of a puzzle than Stefan. Do we even know his full name?'

'According to the papers from Burns, Nicholas Evans, but it seems to be a false name.'

'Why am I not surprised. He was . . . '

Cannon searched for the right words, 'he felt to me like a man with a mission, he was definitely a cut above the usual builder's labourer.'

'It does happen these days,' Helen said, 'the stresses and strains of banking, teaching, social services — the police come to that — can make men head for the joys of simple labouring, — and I don't blame them.'

Cannon stopped walking, a few steps more around the curve of the dunes and they would be in sight of the police at the recovery scene. 'Nor me,' he said, 'suppose I did much the same myself.'

'Well, for Liz, you did,' she corrected him.

'I would have done more,' he said quietly, then shrugged, 'but there's more to this whole affair than a man coming illegally into this country to rescue his sister. These two murders are linked, and that link is the key to that hidden nine-tenths of the iceberg. If we can find Stefan and learn how he and Nick met and how long they had known each other, that would be a start, and — ' But he closed his mouth on the sentiment that Jones would find out nothing by dragging in Hoskins, Stefan, or himself come to that, and treating them as possible murder suspects.

'We don't believe . . . ' she stopped herself, shook her head at him. 'I find it very difficult to treat you as I should, like a general member of the public, because not only do you talk like a policeman, you *feel* like my superior officer.'

He grinned at her, 'Once a policeman . . . but I'll keep out of Jones's hair — if I can.'

'Please do. I'll let you know if we trace Stefan.'

And I'll do the same, he thought as he watched her walk on, then he called after her. 'By the way, when I was in the Stump's Shadow there was talk of a regular who had not been around for a day or two. I just heard his first name, it was Ivo, probably Croatian.'

He felt that the look of 'what-more-are-you-not-telling me' Helen shot him at that moment was much the same as Liz's, when later that morning she found him tearing out the two maps of the fishing pools and the Health Hydro from the county magazine.

'You are not still intending to go?' Liz demanded. 'Another murder and you're still persisting, still risking encountering Jones again.' She put her hands on her hips. 'I tell you what, you deserve to get taken into custody if you do.'

He grinned at her, but she shook her head, refusing to be placated.

'Jones is away in London until later today,' he told her. 'It's my one opportunity to have a look round. If I find anything unusual I shall go straight to Helen, I promise, and that's an end to it.'

'No,' she said, 'there never will be an end to it. You just can't help yourself.'

She had turned away — and that hurt — but the thought of not going was so much worse. 'I'll be as quick as I can,' he promised.

He found that promise was not helped by the fact that although the fishing lakes were nearer than the Health Hydro, he had to drive to the furthest extent of these lakes, which he glimpsed only in bright flashes of sunlit water through dense plantations of conifers, azaleas and rhododendrons. He guessed it must have added some further fifteen kilometres to his journey, before he found an entrance marked 'Fishing Lakes' and inside where the drive divided he could see two fingerposts, one announced 'Fishing Lodge' and the second 'The Chalets.'

He drove past, turned his jeep in the first gateway he found, then back to where he had seen a picnicking area, with tables and parking spaces on the opposite side of the road. He took his jeep in there, parked inconspicuously at the rear of the clearing, then walked back to the Fishing Lodge carrying his fishing gear. He passed two large empty car parks before he came to a large expensive-looking reproduction of a log cabin — here there were five or six vehicles. No doubt in the summer the car parks would be full, but he had expected there to be more on this bright, calm October day.

Cannon went up the steps into what was part-shop and part-office. Every kind of fishing aid, plus clothes, waders, everything a fisherman could desire was on show, and behind a counter sat a middle-aged man, who Cannon was sure was also Portuguese, like the owner, the man who had dominated the Stump's Shadow.

'I can help you?' the man asked.

'I hope so,' Cannon replied, 'I'd like just a day's fishing.'

'Now? Today?'

Cannon nodded, then as the man opened a book of day licences, asked, 'Tell me about your chalets, do you have to book well in advance?'

'In the summer, yes, very early. Now, no problem.' He held out the licence on which he had written the date and the name Cannon had supplied, I. Walton, and said, 'Forty pounds.'

'For fishing?' Cannon queried.

'Forty pounds,' the man repeated.

'Forty,' Cannon echoed, 'you don't get many pensioners fishing here then?'

The man shrugged and struggled with the word he had been instructed to offer. 'Exclusivity,' he said.

This, Cannon thought as he pulled his wallet from his back pocket, was when he truly realized he was unofficial, on his own, no expense account, no reimbursement. 'Any advice about where to find the best sport,' he waved the licence, 'for your money?'

'Ah!' the man smiled and raised a forefinger, 'yes, keep to right, right hand paths.'

'Towards the chalets?' Cannon interrupted.

The man nodded and went on. 'Until you come to very large lake, there is good, that is where the big boss always fish.'

As he walked the paths, flanked by the evergreen shrubs and conifers, it was easy to forget that winter was coming. Screened and sheltered from that fact, he wondered what else all this concealed, and with no warning an icy chill shot up from the base of his spine to prickle the hairs on the back of his neck. Helen Moore would have had an apt quotation for the sensation, he thought, as he walked on, probably something to do with *something wicked this way comes.*

'Exclusivity' was the word that came to his lips as he came to the first pair of chalets. These were more like extensive wooden bungalows, attractively built in a clearing with open aspects of the lakes beyond, each having large decked areas at the back to sit out and admire the surroundings.

It seemed an idealized view as he walked on towards the lake, and this surely must be what the man had called the large lake. As he drew nearer, the water some distance from the bank was disturbed and Cannon realised there was a fisherman over to his right who had just made a magnificent cast way out into the deep waters. He stopped to watch, and as he did the fly was taken, he was near enough now to hear the whirl of the line as it spun from the reel. The fish had well and truly swallowed the bait and in seconds had realized it had more than just a fly in its mouth. The reel screamed as the fish headed off towards the middle of the lake. Cannon began to move to where the unseen fisherman must be standing so he could watch the skill of the angler more closely, the playing of the fish before it was brought inshore. He approved as the line continued to play out, then when the fish turned, the second before the line went dangerously slack, it was quickly reeled in to keep the contact.

He went nearer and could see the outline of the man standing on a small peninsula out into the lake, completely absorbed in his sport. Cannon's own heart quickened as the game continued. Once more the reel screamed as the fish headed off at speed, away towards deeper water. He came up behind the last few shrubs screening the tiny spit of land and was about to call out that the man had a good fish on the end of his line, when he saw that the fisherman was the man from the bar, Vaso de Garro, the owner.

Cannon stepped discreetly away, but stayed near enough to watch the outcome of the battle between man and fish, and now felt a perverse wish the trout, for this he was sure it was, would slip the hook.

But it did not. He admired the man's tenacity, and was convinced he had had such good sport that he would carefully remove the hook and return the trout to the water. From where he watched he saw de Garro pull the fish in close, then deftly push a landing net under it and lift it out — three or four pounds Cannon guessed. A good catch. He saw the stout Portuguese land the fish on the bank, and reach into his bag for, Cannon imagined, his de-gouger to remove the hook without doing damage, but instead of which de Garro brought out a priest, the short heavy club used by fishermen to kill their catch.

So this fish was for the table, he thought, as de Garro raised the metal-ended priest and brought it down on the fish's head — not once, or twice, but three times, then a fury of blows which must have rendered the trout not just dead but uneatable. Cannon had difficulty not intervening, and by the time de Garro had straightened, Cannon realized that not only was he gawping open-mouthed with astonishment, but with the certain knowledge that this man was capable of anything.

He watched as de Garro now repacked his bag, picked up his rod and walked away. Cannon waited until he was out of sight and earshot going towards the far side of the lake, and presumably back to his Health Hydro, then he went to view the fish.

It was, or had been, a handsome rainbow trout, now as torn about as if it had indeed been cooked and eaten from, and the remains left on someone's plate. Cannon found several large dock leaves, picked up the remains, then stooped and pushed them off the bank into the lake. The leaves supported the game fish for a moment, then the body slid beneath the waters. A tiny Viking funeral for a fighter, not a corpse abandoned to flies.

Leaving his fishing kit by the lakeside Cannon followed the path taken by de Garro, and after passing several blocks of chalets found himself on the far side of the lake. Here more ancient oaks, copper beech and banks of rhododendrons had been pleasantly disposed by some landscape gardener generations ago; dense near the periphery, they gradually gave way to neatly manicured lawns near a great Elizabethan mansion. Huge, with large multi-paned windows, a true celebration of glass, it was a splendid building. Cannon was just in time to see de Garro go inside a conservatory which had been added and ran the entire length of the back of the building. He could make out men on loungers in white dressing gowns. De Garro paused by them, then passed out of sight.

Using the trees and shrubs as cover, Cannon made his way further around, wanting to see as much of the place as possible and get as near as he could. He froze as a dog barked, the deep-throated bark of a large animal. A guard dog? The thought was followed by the sight of two men in pale brown uniforms, undoubtedly security, with an alsatian on a short, stout lead. They seemed to be patrolling at the edge of the lawns, in sight of the Hydro and its customers. As he watched they met a similar couple with another dog. They appeared to compare notes for a moment, then they crossed over, each pair continuing on the way the other two had just come from. It seemed extraordinary security for a Health Hydro. He wondered if de Garro carried on other sadistic practices in this heavily guarded Spa — if he could beat a harmless fish to pulp . . .

He had hardly contemplated the fate of anyone, young illegal women immigrants in particular, who fell into this man's power, when to his astonishment he saw the man who had issued his licence at the fishing lodge, emerge from the shrubbery and call out to the security officers. All four men went back to him. Cannon was even more astonished when he saw the man was carrying the fishing gear he had left near the lake, and was displaying it to the guards.

He glanced once more at the elegant building; this place was definitely suspect, but maybe he had done enough scouting for one day. He headed back in the general direction he had come, trying to decide whether to call at the lodge, wait for the assistant's return and report his lost gear. He could say he had left it while he reconnoitred the best place to fish, returned and it was gone. This would be the most normal behaviour for an innocent fisherman, but as to whether it was the most advisable? Perhaps high-tailing it as soon as possible was the best option, but he was reluctant.

He came across another clearing with chalets he had not passed before. He paused in front of these holiday-lets to check he was going in the right direction. It sounded as if the security men had spread out behind him, sweeping the shrubbery, and were rapidly getting nearer.

He looked quickly around for his best way out, then thought he heard a noise from one of the chalets, and, more eerily, had that strange feeling that he was being watched. He glanced at the windows, dismissing the sensation, and was about to plunge down the most likely looking path, when the front door slowly opened, not far, but enough to be an invitation — the noise of the men with their dogs was close . . .

He took one long stride from grass to doorstep to leave no tell-tale damp footprint, was inside, closed the door, heard the yale lock click behind him — and then worried about who else might be in there.

Cannon stood with his back to the door, listened to the men reach the clearing and pass on, then all he could hear was his own breathing. When that and his heart steadied — nothing.

Had he taken refuge with a double murderer, or some vagrant who'd seen Cannon outside, felt a fellowship and offered sanctuary . . . or had it been some freak draught of wind moving a door inadvertently left open. Even for a capricious breeze the timing was too convenient. He cleared his throat and asked, 'Anyone there?'

There was no answer, but this silence felt aware, as if someone was listening. 'Thanks for letting me in,' his voice echoed, sounded much too loud as he added, 'whoever and wherever you are. Thanks.' He moved two steps further into the carpeted hallway. There were four doors off it; the furthest one on his left stood ajar. He moved nearer and could see kitchen units with marble tops, terracotta floor tiles.

'I am coming into the kitchen,' he said and a chair scraped across the tiles and Cannon's nerves. He started, swore, and lurched into the kitchen to face a man clutching the back of a chair until his knuckles shone white. He looked like a tramp; his jacket and jumper were in tatters, and for a moment Cannon did not recognize him.

It was four days since Stefan Tomac had jumped down and run from the loft, five since Nick's murder — and he looked as if he had neither shaved nor eaten since.

'Stefan?'

No reply.

'You opened the door for me,' Cannon said, and when the man did not answer, but just stood staring, gripping the chair back, he added, 'Thanks. Security men with dogs, over the top for this place in the daytime . . . '

Stefan still did not answer.

'How long have you been here?'

'You . . . bring the police?' Stefan's voice sounded thick with disuse.

'No . . . no,' the complexity of why he was there, was too much to explain as yet, and not to a man in this state. 'When did you last eat?' he asked.

'I find blackberries.'

Cannon felt distressed he had nothing to offer this man, except . . . He pushed his hand into his pocket. Stefan backed violently away, lifting the chair, as if to defend himself.

Cannon shook his head — had there been a gun in his pocket the chair would have been little defence. He pulled out his hand and opened it to reveal three mints wrapped in grimy blue paper, which had probably been in his fishing coat since the previous autumn. He put them on the table. 'It's all I have with me.'

Stefan put down the chair and picking one up, attempted to remove the wrapper, but when the end twists just came away, he put the rest into his mouth as it was and worked at it as if desperate for any kind of nourishment.

'I'll get you proper food,' Cannon promised.

Stefan removed some of the sweet paper

from his mouth, and put the other two sweets in his pocket. Cannon sat down, letting him get the sugar into his mouth and system, but looked questioningly at the terrible old jumper and coat he had on.

'From a . . . ' Stefan began, 'in a field.'

'A scarecrow?'

Stefan nodded. 'I walk here at night, across fields,' he said then asked, 'Why *you* come to this place?'

'I was following a lead, a clue,' he began. 'And you? What made you walk all this way? Not just to hide.'

'Police not coming?'

'No.' Cannon sat down. 'The police, the inspector in charge, may still think you have left the country.' He told him of the lorry found at Newhaven and Stefan repositioned the chair at the opposite side of the table and sat down. 'But I was sure you would not leave until you had found your sister. That is why you came, isn't it?'

'For certs,' Stefan said and both men were still, absorbing his use of a phrase Nick had said so often — never 'certainly', always 'for certs'.

'How did you meet Nick?' Cannon asked gently.

A look, something like panic, passed over Stefan's face and he shook his head. 'It was an accident,' he said, frowning, sucking at the last trace of mint in the roof of his mouth.

Cannon did not press him on that point, instead telling him of his visit to the Boston pub, of the man, Ivo, being missing, of the translator who had followed him.'

'Alamat, you spoke to him?' he asked in surprise.

'He told me Ivo worked here as a security guard, and — '

'Yes, Ivo, it is him I want to see again . . . ' There was cold fury in his voice now. He glanced sharply at Cannon, 'You read the letters in my jacket? You know my sister saw this man.'

'Yes,' Cannon nodded, judging it was not time to tell he believed the man pulled from the sea to be this Ivo — the body was not yet officially unidentified. Instead he asked, 'Why were the addresses torn from the tops of the letters?'

'Nick . . . ' Stefan began, then frowned and his manner became guarded.

Cannon was once more convinced there was a lot more to be disclosed, still a lot this man was not telling.

'Stefan,' he said, 'I can only help if you tell me everything.'

'Only proper address on first,' Stefan blurted out.

'Where your sister worked for little or nothing,' Cannon said, adding quietly, 'these people should be punished.'

'Yes,' he said.'

'But?' Cannon queried as he did not go on.

'After I find my sister,' Stefan said with finality.

'Her first employers might have some information as to where she moved to.'

'I think not.' Stefan shook his head, then startled Cannon by dropping his clenched fists hard on the table. 'Find sister first!' he exclaimed.

'OK,' Cannon placated. 'So was it the address on the second letter that made you come here?'

He shook his head. 'No address,' he said, 'I do not think Antonija knew address, knew where she was . . . is. Nick and I go to Stump's Shadow, many times, we meet Ivo, but he . . . ' A look of bitterness crossed his face as he searched for the words, 'he all talk. A man who takes everything, wants every-thing, money, rings, anything, anything, he takes from people, when he says he will help them, but it is only . . . ' He raised his hand and shortened the distance between his forefinger and thumb until it was nothing, 'promises, and,' he looked at Cannon with heart-rending despair in his eyes. 'All

Antonija's letter said was, 'Near sea''.

'So why tear that — ' Cannon began, but Stefan shook his head, and Cannon changed tack. 'So what did you and Nick find out about this Ivo?'

'Only that he worked for,' he threw out his chest as if making himself important, 'de Garro.'

'The man who owns all this and the Hydro, a man who invites the rich and influential to shooting parties on his land,' Cannon said.

'Yes, this Nick find out, and he come here, to the Hydro, and I did not see again.'

Something like an electric shock passed through Cannon. He rose and went to stand motionless staring out of the kitchen window. Nick came here and was then found dead in a ditch, garrotted with a fishing line, his face under a mud-pack, but clothes and shoes immaculate. Mud was part of beauty treatments, and clients took off their clothes, wore dressing gowns.

'When Nick came here, how did he come, secretly, or . . . '

Stefan shook his head. 'He laughed, said he'd tell me when he came back. I was not to worry.'

'We must find your sister,' Cannon said. 'Do you have any evidence she might have been here?'

'I watch, see other girls brought in white van, every night, always between ten and eleven, and sometimes,' he gave Cannon a haunted look, 'take away women and parcels.'

'Parcels? What kind of parcels?'

'In blankets, take two men to carry.'

'My God, what's going on here!' Cannon exclaimed before he had time to think better of it.

'I think we know what happening. Antonija's letter say no good man want her now.'

Then both men raised their heads, listening. It sounded as if the security men were coming back that way and just in time Cannon grabbed Stefan and threw the two of them to the floor near the sink units, so that the man whose bulk darkened the window as he peered in could not see them.

They lay, waited, listened, for a long time, then Stefan whispered, 'You come in Willy jeep, they find that? Nick said only one in area, everyone know who it belong to.'

Cannon shook his head. 'I left it some distance away,' he said.

'Good,' Stefan said, 'so you stay here, watch for tonight's van, help me rescue my sister.'

'I promise,' Cannon said without the least hesitation, 'I'll do everything in my power.'

7

Though she could hardly have expected him back from a real fishing trip for hours and hours yet, Liz let out a gasp of relief, and pleasure, as she heard the unmistakeable agricultural note of Cannon's Willy jeep. Then she wondered why he was swinging into the car park, rather than going straight to the garage . . .

She went out to meet him and ask, but when he saw her coming she thought he looked like a man who needed a little more time to prepare his answers. He returned her greeting, but ignored her question, taking her hand as if she was an unruly child who wanted to know too much, and walked her back to the pub kitchen without a word, or at least not a spoken one. She could imagine there were plenty flashing through his mind. But just like their days together in the Met, he would be trying to format them into some unassailable order, so argument against a decision he had already made, would seem useless.

'So what's so difficult to tell?' she asked. 'What have you done?'

'Done?' For a moment he objected to what sounded like an accusation, then he said, 'I found Stefan and he's starving.'

'Starving as in hungry?' she asked.

He nodded.

'I need to take him food, and — '

'And?'

'I must stay with him, at least for a time tonight. I've rung Paul — he's willing to come over until I get back.'

'Paul!' she exclaimed, 'it would have been nice to be consulted. I was hoping . . . ' she smothered what she had been hoping. She had a long-held ambition to find time to join Paul Jefferson's watercolour class, not to call their mutual friend in as a part-time help and barman, as they often seemed to.

'Paul doesn't mind,' he said, 'he's just finished a landscape for a customer, has promised to deliver that and he'll come straight on here afterwards. It may be a little after opening time, and I need to take Stefan some clothes, and a sleeping bag. Could you pack up some food while — '

'You talk,' she told him, emphasizing, 'I need to know, John.'

'Sure.'

She watched him critically as he prepared to be patient, put-out, but patient.

He sighed. 'Alright, a briefing then.'

'A full briefing,' she said. 'Tell me, first, where you found Stefan.'

The where was quickly told and understood.

'But why are you so certain this place is where — well, where Stefan's sister might be, or have been.'

'Because Nick was looking for her, was on to something and went there. But above all,' he paced a few tense contemplative steps towards the door and back, hands thrust deep in his pockets, 'the way he was murdered. Think of his body, his clothes, his shoes, then think of a customer going to a Health Hydro, of the mud they use, of the treatments when all one has on is a towel.'

'There's something macabre about all this,' she shuddered, 'so he was put back into his clothes after he had been garrotted . . .'

' . . . With a fishing line, next to fishing lakes,' Cannon interrupted, seeing again the line singing out from de Garro's rod, and his mutilated catch afterwards. He told her what he had seen.

She was appalled. 'What man does to helpless things always feels . . .' she began then faltered.

'It's a failure of stewardship,' Cannon stated.

'Yes,' she agreed, 'that's it.' She looked at

108

her man with new respect. He could still surprise her with his beliefs.

'Then something else happened,' he went on, 'as I left the fishing complex and walked along the road to where I left the jeep, I heard a vehicle behind me. I turned to see it was one of new type of window cleaners — carry their own tank of water — and this one was real naff, had a big plastic fireman with hose on top, and the message 'We Wash Dry and Polish' in large letters all over his van. I flagged him down, asked him if he cleaned the windows at the Hydro. He said he had done for some time and immediately produced a card.' Cannon took the white business card, with the fireman and hose logo on it, from his back pocket and spun it on to the kitchen table. 'He obviously thought I was a potential customer, and he was not about to miss any opportunity. He was Slovak, full of himself and his one-man business, until I asked him if he remembered ever posting a letter for a young lady who was at the Hydro. He stopped talking so abruptly his mouth was still sagging open. When I asked again he just said he worked only for the owner, no one else.'

' 'Worked for', suggests . . . '

'He took the money Antonija says she stole to give to the window cleaner,' Cannon nodded agreement, 'and we know someone posted the letter.'

'So you think he was the one?'

'I'm sure. When I still pressed him, he shouted he had told the big man he knew nothing. He nearly took my hand off when he slammed back into his van and I tried to hold on to the door. He sped off as if the hounds of hell were after him.'

'The big man?' Liz queried, picking up the card. 'That could be a big man like Sergeant Maddern.'

'Or a big terrifying man, like de Garro; they're all scared stiff of him, and this little window cleaner was terrified.'

He told her of the van Stefan had seen, sometimes bringing young women, some-times taking them away, he omitted the long heavy blanket-wrapped burdens.

'We should tell Helen,' she stated.

'If there's any kind of police presence at this point he'll be gone, and one thing we do know about Stefan is he's good at running and hiding. I just want to keep faith with him and stay with him a bit, tonight at least.'

'You don't want Jones involved,' she said bluntly.

'No, I don't want him scaring Stefan away. He's in a state, Liz.' Cannon urged, 'Let's get him fed, in some warm clothes, then I'll be able to think how to play this. I'll be careful — the sooner I go, the sooner I'll be back.'

'I seem to have heard that before,' Liz said, getting up and taking a large vacuum flask from the cupboard. 'Soup for a start I would think. You mustn't let him have too much too quickly.'

'No, and I'll take half a bottle of brandy — a little of that won't hurt either.'

In less than half an hour she saw him off again with a haversack of food and a roll of bedding and clothes. He threw these in the back of the jeep, turned to face her, and for a moment there was too much to say, only silence served.

'Take care,' she said.

'I will,' he pulled her into his arms. 'I'll phone you,' he said, 'give you a progress report.'

'What do I tell Paul, if he asks?'

'Perhaps just that it's about the builders,' he suggested.

'He'll guess you're up to no good.'

'I think good's just what I am up to,' he said nodding down at her.

'I know you do, that's always our problem.'

She stood and watched him drive away, careful not to shake her head until he had given her a final wave and was out of sight. It was suddenly chilly and lonely out there. She glanced at her watch — another half an hour to opening time. She rather hoped one of the regulars would be in early.

In fact it was a stranger who walked in.

She had just finished piling the logs on the open fire in the bar, which she would light later, when the man walked in. He was not tall, but had an air of bulky, slightly swaggering, strength about him. 'Allow me,' he said, flicking a cigarette lighter from his overcoat pocket and putting the flame to the newspaper protruding from the kindling, under the logs.

'Thanks,' she said, trying to keep the irony from her voice and returning to the business side of the bar, asked 'what can I get you?'

'Any chance of something to eat?'

If she momentarily wondered about leaving this stranger alone while she prepared something, this was immediately alleviated by the arrival of Billy Brompton, a sling around his neck, into which as he came into the bar he inserted his heavily bandaged right arm.

'Billy?' she questioned, 'what's happened?'

'The usual,' he replied, 'the wife. Seven stitiches. Give us a pint, Liz.

'Can I get you a drink as well,' she asked her first customer, 'while you look at the bar menu?'

'I'll have a pint, as well,' he said, reaching into his back pocket, 'and let me pay for this gentleman's. If he has a wife like that I reckon he deserves a treat.'

'Ah! Don't you get it wrong, mate,' Billy put in. 'I love my Madge, it's just when I provoke her when she's got something in her 'and.'

'What was it this time,' Liz asked.

'The shovel,' he said, 'she was sweeping up outside.'

'The course of true love,' the stranger said, 'never runs smooth.'

'Where you from, then?' Billy asked, 'London or thereabouts?'

'Work in London, but hail from near Birmingham originally. Keith Brand the name, and you?'

The introductions made all round, Brand said, 'I can see your next question coming. What am I doing here? Two things really, having a break and looking up an old colleague of mine, Nick Evans.'

The stunned silence was broken by a log shifting in the grate. Billy looked at it and said, 'You've lit the fire early, Liz.'

'Ah!' Brand acknowledged his untimely help on that score, but looking from one to the other, questioned their altered expressions, their gazes that dropped away as he met them. 'You've heard of Nick? You know him?'

Liz nodded and Billy said, 'You're in for a bit of a shock, mate.'

'Your Nick Evans, was he a builder?' Liz asked.

'Oh he does all kinds of things, nothing would surprise me.'

'I think this will,' Billy said.

It was a stunned man some twenty minutes later who stood rigid and pale, his untouched meal before him.

'The murder was front page in our local newspaper,' Billy said, 'but not his name though, I wondered about that.'

Brand glanced at him and shook his head. 'These days a country murder doesn't often make more than a few lines in the nationals . . . and without a name, it wasn't picked up.'

Billy gave a humph of disgust. 'I should have thought this one might, it was . . . '

'Was?' Brand appeared to snap out of shock into impatience and anger. 'Was what?'

'Well there was plenty of local gossip,' Billy said.

'There were some strange circumstances which the police suppressed,' Liz said, 'for the obvious reasons.'

'Obvious?' Billy questioned.

'Circumstances which only the murderer would know, often helps in cross-questioning,' Liz spelled out. 'The murderer can give himself away by knowing more than has been made public.'

'So how do you know there were strange circumstances?' Brand asked.

'Liz's partner found the body,' Billy supplied.

'That will be John Cannon then,' Brand said, 'I saw the names above the pub door. If you are Liz, Liz Makepeace, then your partner presumably is . . . '

'Right.'

'So is Mr Cannon about?'

'No.' Liz felt Billy glance at her, the denial was too abrupt, she was in danger of giving too much away herself if she was not careful.

'Be about later?' Brand was asking as the bar door was pushed open and Paul Jefferson walked in.

'Hi!' he greeted Liz, 'earlier than I thought. Old boy gone?'

Liz nodded, and as Paul's eyes fell on Billy's bandaged arm resting on the counter, the sling round his neck, he exclaimed, 'Not Mad Irish Madge again!'

Billy shrugged, then as Paul nodded to the newcomer, Billy went on to introduce Keith Brand and explain he had arrived looking for his friend, Nick . . .

'You mean you hadn't heard?' Paul asked. 'My God what a shock for you.'

'Indeed,' Brand agreed, but now seemed somewhat constrained by the presence of the

115

urbane and casually elegant Paul, and rose, saying, 'I must make one or two phone calls. He walked out of the bar and stood outside the front windows, pulling out his mobile, tapping the keys, then as he put it to his ear he walked out of sight.

'Doesn't want us to hear,' Billy commented.

'Could be quite upsetting, telling someone who knows Nick, maybe even related to him,' Paul suggested.

Liz did not answer, remembering that John had told her the murdered man's identity had not been traced by the police, and the name, Nicolas Evans, believed to be false — but it seemed it was the one Brand had known his friend by.

'What does he do, do you know?' Paul asked nodding his head towards the man outside.

'Something about him that takes a bit of fathoming,' Billy said.

'He's built like a small bull, but his quick sharp glances have the craftiness of a fox,' Paul mused.

'You'd best paint a picture,' Billy said, 'you've lost me.'

'So where's this chap of yours gone,' Paul asked Liz.

'To see a man about a builder,' she was

saying as Brand came back inside, unzipping his coat.

'Oh! Well, whatever,' Paul answered, 'I can stop until he gets back.'

'It could be late,' she told him.

'No problem,' he replied.

Brand strode to the end of the bar taking his bar snack with him, and began to eat stolidly, with the air of a man who had made a decision and was now sitting out time before putting it into action.

The evening wore on, slowly, and apart from making up one or two bar snacks, Liz could have managed very well on her own. But with a pub you never knew; could be a bus load arrive, or half a dozen people wanting eats all at once, and Paul's was a comforting presence — particularly with Brand now sitting silent, but watchful, in Hoskins's usual pew seat at the end of the bar.

'This should liven things up,' Paul whispered to her and nodded to the door. For the first time since his thorough dousing in the sea Hoskins walked into the bar.

'About time, you old bugger,' someone greeted him from a corner near the fire. 'Got anything for me?'

'Tomorrow,' Hoskins said walking directly towards his seat. The dozen or so regulars held their breath.

'You're in my seat,' Hoskins said as Liz pulled his usual pint.

'Right,' Brand prepared to get up, then still sitting on the edge added, 'so you're a regular, know everything around here I shouldn't wonder.'

'You a copper?' Hoskins said waving him impatiently out of his place.

'Don't you like the police?' Brand asked and there were guffaws from the bar.

'He's their right-hand man,' someone called. 'Fetch him in to help.'

'Wouldn't be the first time,' Hoskins retaliated.

Liz moved defensively to that end of the bar, ready to support Hoskins's claim to the seat, but as Brand stood up, put his hand in his pocket and paid for the old boy's pint, she felt even more alarmed. Hoskins goaded by mention of his arrest, then placated by a stranger who paid for his drink, could be a dangerous mix. Hoskins was likely to say far too much, and could easily reveal that he knew more about recent events than he ought to.

'Where's the boss,' he asked as he sat down.

'Out for a while,' Liz said.

'Not an away darts match, where's he gone?' Hoskins persisted.

'Gone to see about some builders,' Paul said.

'Let's hope they're luckier than the last two he had,' Hoskins said, draining half his glass.

'You knew Nick and Stefan?' Brand asked.

'Talked to them in 'ere,' Hoskins replied, putting his empty glass on the counter with a thump. Brand nodded to Liz, who wanted to object, but didn't know quite how at that point, though with the third refill she did caution Brand that the man he was plying with drink had to ride his pushbike home at closing time.

It became increasingly obvious that Keith Brand intended to stay on until the last, hoping no doubt to talk to John, particularly after Hoskins had revealed that Liz and John were former Met officers. He had regarded her with new interest and shortly afterwards had once more disappeared outside. He came back in folding his phone, with, she thought, an air of satisfaction, of having learnt something significant.

She felt even more anxious for him to leave. She had been surprised when he had mentioned Stefan's name linked to Nick's. Did he, too, know far more than he was saying?

Billy and several of his friends had began a friendly darts match, Billy throwing with his left hand, which caused hilarity, and then consternation as arrows first pinged the light shade above the board, then ricocheted and landed back near the thrower's feet. 'I think you should desist, old boy,' Paul called from behind the bar.

'He means stop!'

'Before you kill somebody,' another echoed, quickly amending this to 'before you hurt somebody.'

'Time you all went home anyway,' a new voice came from behind the counter.' Paul and Liz had been so engrossed with the flying darts they had not seen John come in from the back. 'It's gone eleven o'clock,' he added, 'fine lot of deputies I've got.'

Paul grinned at him, but then asked, 'you OK?'

John nodded but Liz saw he looked as if he'd had a harrowing time.

'I'll get off then, if you're sure there's nothing else I can do.'

'No, and thanks a lot, I'll — ' John began but Paul waved whatever he was going to say aside.

'I'll come and dine at your expense some time,' he said.

The bar began to empty. John saw Hoskins stagger a little as he got up, and in spite of looking completely shattered, Liz heard him offer to put the bike in the back of the jeep and run him home.

'You will not, you're forever hauling me about,' Hoskins retorted, and made for the door.

'I'll see him off then,' John said, and, nodding to Keith Brand, said, 'see you out too, sir.'

To Liz's relief Brand nodded and preceded John and Hoskins out of the door. She had nearly finished the final sweep for dirty glasses and was placing the final half dozen on the counter when she heard voices and turned to see John and Keith Brand walk back in. She scowled at John, who ignored her as he invited Brand through to their kitchen, calling back over his shoulder, 'Lock up, love.'

'Yes sir,' she mouthed, then having done that, checked the fire was safe and put out the lights, she marched through to the kitchen and demanded, 'So what's going on?'

'I think we need to hear what this gentleman has to say before we go any further,' John said pulling out another chair for her at the table.

'I don't understand,' Liz began.

'No, neither do I as yet,' John said, 'but . . . ' he extended a hand to their visitor.

'Keith Brand,' he supplied.

'. . . has just told me that he is a journalist, and — '

'So was my friend Nick.'

'Nick, our builder,' Liz wanted to be ultra sure of the facts.

'Nick was working here as a journalist, an investigative journalist, which was his job,' Brand said, then added, 'Look, it'll probably be easier and quicker if I tell you how Nick and Stefan met.'

They both nodded.

'Nick was on the M1 making his way up to the Midlands on a designer goods scam story, when he decided to take a break at the Leicester service station. It was busy and as he looked for a parking spot a man leapt over the grass verge separating the lorry park from the car park and ran straight in front of him. Nick was only at a crawl, but he still knocked this man down. Nick wanted to get medical help, but the man looked more likely to run across the motorway itself to escape, than to hang around for any kind of assistance. Nick kept hold of his arm after helping him up, he'd guessed from his clothes and his grubby unshaven state that he was probably an illegal immigrant escaping from the back of one of the lorries. He also guessed he was hungry.'

Cannon shot a glance at Liz which seemed to say, nothing new there then.

'Nick suggested he wait while he parked the car and then he'd buy him one of those huge all-day breakfasts and as much coffee as he could drink. He just couldn't turn the offer down, and as he ate he opened up, told Nick a story about coming over to save his sister from the proverbial fate worse than death.' Brand laughed, but neither John nor Liz responded.

'Well, Nick always has — had — a nose for a story. He called into the office, spoke to me first, then was put through to the editor to tell him he was diverting to a story which had more potential. The boss knew him well enough to trust his judgement and gave him leave to carry on, just to send something as soon as he could.'

'And?' Cannon said.

'Nick had a habit of never revealing his story until he was sure of his ground, and had it pretty well sewn up. There was just one message to say it was something big, together with the name of this pub, where he said he was working with this illegal immigrant, Stefan, but time has gone on and . . . '

'You've been sent to find out what he was doing,' Cannon concluded.

'To find he's dead, murdered.' Brand lowered his head, making him look more bull-like than ever. 'It's been a sobering evening; all I know is my friend and colleague is dead, murdered in strange circumstances, which suggests that someone found out who he was and silenced him, and that you found the body,' he stopped and looked speculatively at Cannon, then added, 'no, that's not true, I also know who you both are. The old man, Hoskins, gave me a clue and a call to my newspaper's librarian did the rest.'

They were both silent, reassessing all that had happened in the light of this new knowledge.

'But there's one other thing,' Brand said, his voice low and deep with intent, 'I'm going to carry on where Nick left off.'

8

It was two o'clock in the morning when Liz and John were finally alone in their bedroom, with Keith Brand settled in their spare room.

'When this is all over,' Cannon said as he pulled his t-shirt over his head, 'we'll get that Croatian interpreter in as a handyman, give you time to paint, go to Paul's classes.'

'Are you trying to pacify me?' Liz exclaimed, then remembering their guest in the next bedroom lowered her voice. 'Do you think I'm bothered about that now, when you and . . . ' she flung a hand towards the dividing wall 'are going off tomorrow, probably risking your lives, but sounding like boy scouts going to camp?' She turned on him, furious, fists clenched.

'Hey! Hey!' he breathed, pulling her to him, but she would not be stilled.

'You're a publican, not a policeman or an evangelist, or a bloody investigative reporter . . . ' she tailed off, drumming her fists ineffectively as he held her close, and until, in spite of herself, she leant into his warmth, slipped into her familiar place, her shoulder under his armpit.

'I hate . . . ' she began.

He pushed her away, far enough to look down into her eyes. 'What?'

'Why?' she questioned. 'You'll get no laurels.'

'I'll get justice, or . . . '

She completed the phrase in her head, or die in the attempt. 'John,' she pleaded, 'this idea — we're not going to find yet another body in a ditch somewhere.'

'No, no, Keith just wants to meet Stefan first, and then — '

'*He* wants a scoop,' she said as she pulled away from him and got into bed. 'He doesn't want the police involved until he has his story,' she said more forcefully now she could smother her voice with the duvet, 'but what's in it for you?'

'I wasn't expecting there to be anything in it for me,' he said as he climbed into bed beside her.

'No,' she conceded, ashamed she had even thought such a thing. John wanting something just for himself, she had never known it happen yet.

'In any case I can't leave Stefan stranded and Keith badly wants to learn all he can about Nick's time with him, and then . . . '

'He intends to do exactly what you think Nick did,' she carried on, 'go to the Hydro as a customer, a businessman needing a break?'

Cannon slipped his arm under her and

drew her to him. 'That's the idea.'

'I — '

'Don't you think we've talked enough?' he asked, his hand in the valley of her waist as she lay on her side. Then he raised himself up to kiss below her ear.

'I'm not letting you off,' she said.

'No, of course not,' but he heard the softening note of acquiescence.

Later he murmured, 'Only you.'

'Only me?' she asked from the edge of sleep.

'Yes, you were what I wanted.'

Their alarm woke them at seven. Liz woke to bright sun, and wondered for a moment why she felt so apprehensive. John swung himself up to sit on the side of the bed and she remembered. She was torn between throwing her arms around him, pulling him backwards to her, or giving him a resounding thump. Then she recalled his words 'only you' and sighed.

He turned to looked at her.

I'll fetch some tea,' she said and slipped out of bed.

Before she got to the kitchen she heard pots clattering and entering found Keith already dressed, with his two bags standing at the back door, and the kettle boiling. He was just placing two more mugs on the table.

'Good morning,' he said, 'I heard you coming down.'

'Morning.' She nodded towards the bags. 'You leaving us?'

'Yes,' he replied unequivocally, 'I am going over to Boston early, find a hotel where I can book in and leave my things. If anything should go wrong, I don't want anything found here, making life more complicated for you.'

She could have said quite a lot, could have ranted, raved, threatened, but she stifled everything and just said, 'Thanks.'

'Not an easy man to live with,' he said with a gentle understanding his dark beetle-brows and physical bulk made unexpected.

'Not easy to live up to,' she corrected, as she picked up the two mugs of tea he had made.

'I'm good at breakfasts,' Keith told her, 'am I allowed to get it ready?' He opened the fridge. 'Full English for three?'

Over breakfast it was arranged that Keith would go and arrange his hotel, have a telephone briefing with his editor, then come back to The Trap. The two of them would then go to the fishing complex to see Stefan.

When Keith had gone Cannon said he was going to ask Paul to come over again. 'If he's just finished a painting he's usually at a bit of a loose end,' and before she could raise the matter he added, 'then I'll ring his usual art supply shop and repeat his last order of paints, he won't refuse those.'

'You could ask the proprietor if she thinks he needs anything else, anything he's not bought for a time,' Liz said.

'Will do,' he said lifting the phone which was answered in seconds.

'Paul.'

'Hello, old boy.'

'Are you busy today?'

'No, want me to come over, no problem, pleased to come.'

'If you could give a hand over lunchtime, and early evening, I shouldn't be late back.' He felt he owed Paul some further explanation but as he began Paul cut him off.

'No,' he said sharply, 'don't tell me anything, I don't want to know.'

Cannon frowned as he put down the phone. He and Paul had shared some pretty serious confidences in the past. Paul was good company, he could be flippant, enjoyed a gossip, but like Cannon, had always been able to turn a blind eye to a transgression when it was for the greater good. His refusal to want to hear what was going on was surprising to say the least.

Keith was back by twelve, and greeted

Paul, who had been there about an hour, like an old friend.

Cannon watched the artist's face, waiting for the questions, but none came. He was more sure than ever that there was a reason for this abstemious behaviour, but for now it suited him that the questions were not asked — with others in the bar it could have been awkward.

'I have to pick up some things from the kitchen,' Cannon said.

'I'll wait for you in the car park; we'll take my car,' Keith said.

Paul watched and listened with suspicious interest, but said nothing.

Liz followed to the kitchen, then helped John carry two haversacks of food supplies out to the journalist's black Mercedes.

'How long can you keep Stefan going like this?' the journalist voiced Liz's thoughts.

'I can't force him out, unless I turned him over to the police,' Cannon said, 'and as things stand I won't do that, but you can talk to him, convince him he's got help, he's not on his own.'

'Now my newspaper are going along with this, they'll find him a safe refuge for as long as it takes,' Keith said.

'So they're prepared to do that?' Liz mused aloud.

'You'd be surprised what they'll do,' Keith said, 'the *Daily Endeavour*'s never had a journalist murdered on a job before.'

'Must be like when we, I mean, the police, lose one of their own: no effort spared, no holds barred,' she said and looked up in time to catch the grin on Cannon's face.

'There you go,' Keith added, 'once a police lady always a — '

'Just go,' she said.

'See you later.' Cannon kissed her cheek and got into the passenger seat. She stood and watched the car swing out, disappear, but was not quite ready to go in and face Paul and the few locals in the bar. She went to the tap at the side of the building, unhooked the hose and spent some time watering and dead-heading the pansies. Gardening, even in tubs and baskets, had become a therapy she had learned to value when they had first moved to the Fens.

When she went back in Paul was playing dominoes with three pensioners, friends since school days, who often walked from nearby Reed St Clements when the weather was good, had a pint or two then walked home.

The usual routine, when Paul helped in the mornings, was that Liz would make him lunch, then he would go home, ten minutes' drive away . . . returning about seven. Today, however, when the customers departed, he refused lunch.

'In fact,' he said, 'I think I should tell you something,' he looked at her a little uncertainly, 'and I'm not sure quite how you will take this, but . . . '

'But? Come on, Paul, this is not like you,' she tried to make light of the situation.

'I'm . . . seeing someone,' he said, 'quite seriously seeing someone.'

'Well, wonderful, John will be delighted, he's always said what you need is a good wife.'

'Not so sure he will . . . I mean — '

'Oh we can't always rely on your good nature at the drop of a hat. John was talking about having permanent help once the stable conversion is finished and we have — '

'No,' he interrupted, 'you don't understand. I'm seeing Helen, Helen Moore.'

Liz stared at him. 'Chief Inspector Helen Moore?'

'Yes,' he said, 'so if John's off on one of his missions with that — '

'Friend of Nick's' she supplied.

'That man, Brand, a friend of the builder who was — ' Paul's interest was aroused in spite of himself. 'He looks even less like a builder than Nick did.'

'They weren't builders,' she said, 'they — '

132

'No, no, no!' he exclaimed. 'Don't you see what an awkward position you'll put me in if you tell me anything the police don't already know?'

The sound of a car swinging on to the gravelled car park made them both pause.

'Late customer,' Paul said.

'Too late,' Liz agreed, but wondered if it was John and Keith come back for something they'd forgotten. She walked to the kitchen door and opened it, then turned back to Paul. 'It's your girlfriend,' she said.

It was hardly the right word for the smart uniformed figure of Chief Inspector Helen Moore who strode purposefully towards Liz.

'Hi, Liz,' she greeted her informally. 'Everything all right.' It was not a question. 'I'm the vanguard, Inspector Jones is following on.'

Liz saw the other two exchange glances, but not, she noted, greetings as if they had already seen each other that day, and that anything they said might be construed as evidence. They both looked at her, and the feeling she had was like being one of those coloured fragments in a kaleidoscope. She had not changed, they had not changed, but their relationships with each other had undergone a good shake up.

'Is John here?' Helen asked, 'I rather

wanted to speak to him.'

She might have been going to say, 'before Inspector Jones arrives', but at that moment they heard another car stop outside.

'No,' Liz said, 'he's out, with a friend, who came over from Boston.'

There was no visible sound or reaction but she *felt* Paul stop himself commenting.

They could hear Inspector Jones approaching, his footsteps like the regular pounding of a slow drum — from gravel to grass, to slabs, nothing changed the beat.

'I wanted to let John know that the man he pulled from the sea has been identified as one Ivo Levak, and our forensic scientist has confirmed that the blood in the sand was from the same man.'

'So he was shot, taken off the beach by boat and dumped at sea,' Liz said, 'this was what John thought.'

'He was right,' Helen was confirming, as Inspector Jones arrived on the doorstep, stood and surveyed the three of them, then sucked his teeth before speaking.

'Ma'am, with your permission,' he said to his Chief Inspector, then nodded towards Liz, 'could I speak to your partner,' he said.

'He is not here,' she answered.

'Both your vehicles are,' he said. 'Not off jogging around again?'

'He's out with a friend, in his car.'

'When will he be back?' he asked.

'I didn't give him a time limit,' Liz said shortly.

'So this 'friend', is he an old friend?' Jones asked.

Liz felt this was now amounting to a cross-examination. 'He's from London,' she said, and saw him make the assumption they had known Brand since the time they were in the Met. She also caught a quick glance from Helen and added, 'He's staying in Boston.' She was amazed on two counts, how easy she found it to tell white lies to cover John's tracks, and how loyal and torn their friend Paul must feel, standing between herself and Helen, saying nothing.

'I have told Liz that the body John pulled from the sea, has been identified,' Helen Moore said, 'as has the blood in the sand.'

'Now seems a good time to put another question to Ms Makepeace,' Jones said, the formal title distancing *him* from any personal involvement with the pub landlady, and turning to Liz asked, 'Do you use any kind of facial mud-pack?'

Liz, surprised by this question, did not answer immediately.

'So do you?' he persisted.

'I have done,' she said, 'I do from time to

135

time, irregular intervals you might say.'

'Do you have such a face pack in the house at the moment?'

'Well, yes, I send for them from a firm on the internet who specialize in Black Sea products.'

'I'd like to see them,' Jones said.

She glanced at Helen who inclined her head a fraction. Liz went upstairs to their bathroom. She had not asked why, but the word mud had brought back John's description of Nick's body.

She carried down the box containing seven sealed sachets left from the box of ten she had sent for. Jones held out his hand, but before she passed them over she said, 'I should like to know why you are asking me for these?'

'The forensic scientist,' Helen Moore said before Jones could, 'has analysed the mud from the face of the body found in the ditch, and identified it as a commercial product . . . containing Black Sea mud.'

'We're anxious to trace any such product lying about this area,' Jones emphasized heavily.

'Lying about,' she protested, then her heart thumped as she thought, lying about within a stone's throw of where Nick's body had been found — by John.

Helen Moore added, 'We are also looking

into a Hydro some forty miles away who include such treatments in their brochure.'

Liz's concern about her own mud packs vanished as Jones responded.

'Yes, ma'am, I should go. You don't mind if I take these,' he said to Liz, hardly waiting for her nod before he turned his back on her and moved closer to speak confidentially to his chief inspector. Liz, all inhibitions put aside by mention of the Hydro, moved closer and heard the end of his sentence, ' . . . Some distance to find a magistrate who was willing to sign. We're all laid on for this evening.'

'I have to see the Chief Constable at four,' Helen Moore told him, 'but I'll be there.'

Liz remembered that the owner of the Hydro was said to regularly entertain the local hierarchy at his game shoots and dinner parties. If a search warrant was involved, Jones might have had to travel out of the county to find a magistrate willing to sign. She wondered if there had been stirring of disquiet at the highest level. She remembered a time in her own police days when a whole bench of magistrates had pushed their chairs back when a certain Lady known to them all had stepped into the dock.

The three cars left one after the other, Jones first, then Helen, finally Paul, who promised to be back before the evening opening time. The haste of his departure made Liz feel he and Helen might well both be heading for the same place: Paul's cottage.

She locked the door after them, leaned back on it and pulled out the mobile she had been fingering for long enough in her trouser pocket. She pressed the first name on her contact list. It took that heart-achingly long moment that mobiles do, to begin to ring out — and ring out. There was no answer and she wondered if she had ever felt quite so alone in all her life.

9

When they arrived near the fishing complex, and the spot where Cannon had parked his jeep the day before, they found a mini bus disgorging a party of laughing, chatting, elderly men and women, some already using the picnic seating to change into walking boots.

Brand drove on until they came to a second parking bay a mile or so further on. 'Will this do?' he asked.

'If we could get over that,' Cannon nodded to the substantial fence topped with strands of razor-wire, 'we should be about level with the chalets, and avoid the man in the fishing lodge.'

'Nil desperandum,' Brand said as he swung the car in. 'I've learned a trick or two from a friend who's a photographer for one of these celeb magazines.'

'Specializing in catching the famous unawares,' Cannon commented.

'Right,' Brand confirmed, the enthusiasm in his voice brought back Liz's boy scout comparison.

Brand had his door partly open when a car travelling at excessive speed described a wide and erratic course around the corner they had just travelled.

'I'd have him in my book,' ex-cop Cannon commented, but then instinctively sank down in his seat as the grey limousine swept past, and added, 'That was de Garro!'

'Buggeration!' Brand exclaimed. 'Did he see you?'

'He looked too bloody furious to even see which way the road curved,' Cannon said. 'Wonder how far he'll get, and what's upset him?'

'OK,' Brand said, 'so the big cat's away.'

Cannon followed him to the boot of the car. Brand pulled out a black bag about half a metre square and a thick hessian sack. 'Get the haversacks,' he said.

He crossed the road to the fence, unzipped the bag and brought out a very neat collapsible aluminium ladder, which he extended and locked. 'We can just jump down the other side, but one of us has to balance on the top long enough to raise the ladder after us.'

'I'll do that,' Cannon said and moved the ladder a couple of metres to where the fence was supported by a stout post on the inside.

Brand took the sack and climbed the ladder with more agility than might be expected from a man of his build. At the top he opened out the sacking to cover the wire, then indicated Cannon should pass him the haversacks. These were dropped carefully down the other side, then Brand put one foot on the sacking, collapsing the wire down under his weight and stepped over into space. He's done that before, was Cannon's thought as he heard him land, and followed. At the top of the ladder he pushed one foot under the wire on to the fence post, put his other knee on the sacking pad, so he was standing and half kneeling. In his pocket, his phone vibrated. He paused an extra second to ignore it and rebalance, pulled up the light ladder and passed it over to Brand, who repositioned it on the other side. Cannon stepped on to it, appreciating for the first time that the pad over the razor wire had a stout braid strip to enable him to pull it free of the vicious blades. These items from the car boot were not casual items kept in case needed sometime; they were serious, well-adapted, aids to do a job. He wondered what else was in that boot. Brand was undoubtedly one of those no-holds-barred investigative professionals that could drive policemen — proper, official, policemen — nuts.

Cannon thought of the missed call as Brand was collapsing the ladder which made a click, and immediately both started as a great squarking, flapping, clatter came towards them — a pheasant flew in clumsy panic low over their heads.

They stood rigid, listening, and then crouched in the bushes as they heard voices: two men chatting amiably, but not in English. As they drew nearer, one made a remark which made the other roar with laughter. Their voices grew a little fainter, then they separated, calling last remarks to each other, and still laughing. Cannon was almost sure one of them was the man from the fishing lodge, and he momentarily regretted his confiscated fishing gear.

'What's annoyed the boss, seems to have amused the staff,' Brand whispered.

'Let's get to Stefan, see if he knows what's going on,' Cannon said and began to lead the way to the chalet where he had left the Croatian the night before. Cannon tapped the door, then cupping his hands around his mouth he stooped to the letterbox. 'It's John Cannon,' he said.

The door opened immediately to reveal a man in an extreme state of anxiety. Stefan's black hair stood out at all angles as if he had run his hands frantically through it time and time again, and his eyes were full of trouble.

'Thank God you come,' he said, then saw Brand and stepped back, the other two followed him in, and Brand closed the door. Stefan looked more alarmed.

'No, no,' Cannon said making calming gestures. 'This is a friend of Nick's, another reporter from the same newspaper.'

'I'm going to carry on where Nick left off,' Brand told him, 'bring these bastards to justice.'

Stefan still looked both desperate and bewildered.

'What's happened here?' Cannon prompted.

'After you gone, I slept, warm,' he paused to put his hand on his stomach, giving Cannon a look of gratitude, 'but something woke me. I went out and heard an engine.' He stared at Cannon with eyes that held horror and disbelief. 'The van comes, taking girls away, once, twice, three times, maybe more, I don't know.' His voice dropped almost below hearing. 'I think I saw Antonija. She tried to run away, but they grabbed her arm, I — '

'Your sister,' Cannon said, 'you saw her?'

'Yes, yes, I am sure, but what I do? Nothing!' His hands went up into his hair. 'There were the guards, and other men, and they kept bringing the girls. Some walked, others,' he flung an arm out as if striking a blow. 'One cried out, and — ' the arm went out more violently, 'she was knocked down and lifted into the van.'

'The same van kept coming back?' Cannon asked.

'Yes, but not front way. It come . . . ' his hands described a path around a building, ' . . . and back, and back.'

'It was the same van each time?' Cannon asked again, 'How long was it gone?'

'Minutes. Ten minutes — and yes, same van. By light from doorway I see long scratch on driver's door.' Stefan was certain, his gestures describing a vehicle backing.

'So wherever they took these girls was not far,' Cannon said, 'allowing for unloading, handing them over to whoever was at the other end, then coming back for another load. I'd like to have a good look round these grounds.'

'I try to see this morning,' Stefan said, 'but many people about. But strange, the guards going away, and then cleaners come in vans.'

'He's being thorough,' Cannon said.

'I'd like to get inside as soon as possible,' Brand said, 'have a look round, talk to the staff.'

Stefan shot him a look of concern. 'I think it is what Nick did,' he said, 'all full of . . . ' he searched for the word,

' . . . Confidence,' Cannon supplied.

' . . . yes, but then you find him in ditch. It

is enough, no more killings . . . no more bodies in ditches.'

Or in the sea, Cannon thought.

'Nick was my friend, my good friend,' Stefan wailed.

'And mine,' Brand said darkly, 'and there are these other girls, as well as your sister. My paper means to nail these bastards. Put yourself in my hands, Stefan; when someone murders a colleague neither I nor our newspaper gives up. You have help now, trust me.'

Stefan looked to Cannon, who knew there was more than altruism involved, there was a national newspaper with circulation figures to worry about, but willing to put in funds. Cannon nodded and was saying, 'I think it is the best chance we have of rescuing Antonija quickly,' when his phone vibrated in his pocket again. 'My partner,' he said as he opened it up.

'Hi!' he said, 'yes, yes, we're with him now.' He glanced at Stefan, then listened intently, snapping questions at intervals: 'When?' 'Who said?' 'Time?', and finally, 'Right, I'll keep you posted.' He folded the phone.

'We have to get out of here,' he said, refastening the rucksack he had just undone, as he told them of the coming search. 'We've not much time.'

'We shouldn't leave any trace that anyone's

been here,' Brand said, putting dirty mugs away in a cupboard, 'and I must contact my editor.'

There was an enthusiasm in his voice, an excitement. The reckless boy scout? Cannon wondered.

'He wants to do Nick's disappearance, accidental meeting with immigrant desperate to find his sister, as a lead asap,' Brand went on, 'then hopefully the whole story with the culprits being brought to justice.'

'Courtesy of the *Daily Endeavour*,' Cannon commented, unable to quite keep the cynicism from his voice, 'hope it all goes as smoothly as that. The activity here suggests,' he paused to bundle up the sleeping-bag, 'the evidence might have been whipped away, or wiped clean.'

'So . . . ' Brand began, but Cannon already had a plan.

'What I'd like you to do is take Stefan to the refuge you said you could arrange, but first I want you to drop me at the far boundary of this place. I want to see if there are some clues as to where these girls are, or even just tyre tracks to show the way they went — four or five journeys over the same ground should have left some evidence.'

'OK, but it'll take some time to get Stefan to a safe house.'

'I'll call a taxi when I'm ready to go home, I've numbers on my mobile,' Cannon told him, adding, 'but I should have your number, and Stefan hasn't got a mobile.'

'I'll see to that,' Brand said.

Stefan suddenly seemed very reluctant to leave the chalet, then expressed a wish to go with Cannon, but he was hardly the most stable man to have at one's side at that moment. 'I think you've gone through enough for the time being,' Cannon said, as he made a final check that they had removed all visible traces of anyone having been in the chalet. Stefan shook his head but said no more as laden with rucksacks and a bedding roll, they began the return journey the way Cannon and Brand had come.

Once in the car it took Brand only minutes to drive to where the fence with the razor-wire dropped away towards the coast. 'Good luck,' he said as Cannon got out and glanced at the figure slumped in the back seat, woolly hat pulled down low concealing the wild black hair, but with a growth of stubble too long to be designer and too short to be a beard.

'Get him a shave,' he said to Brand, 'he looks like a brigand.'

Brand grinned, swept the car round, and was away.

Cannon watched them go, then checking there was no one in sight set off across the grass verge, into the field next to the fence. He went quickly along the side, until he came to where it turned left to form the back boundary.

The mansion stood on a slight rise, some half a mile back from the beach, though this was hidden by low dunes and high growths of marram grasses. A minor public road ran between the estate and the dunes. It was very quiet, no wind, no sound from the distant ocean, no clamour of gulls, no honking of geese, and for a moment Cannon felt a childish nostalgia for the roar of London traffic, and the lavish Cockney welcome from his gran in Bow.

'Christ,' he breathed. He was feeling as if this was a momentous thing he was about to do, as if he was going into battle! He'd had these apprehensive moments of biting off more than he could chew before. The trouble was he was usually right. He forced his mind back to the task he'd set himself, to evidence he could see, for God's sake, not just sense like some sea anemone trawling the waters.

It was obvious that not a lot of traffic passed through this narrow road, for the verges on either side were unmarked by vehicles having to pull in tight to the sides to allow each other to pass — and so far there was no sign of a back way to the Hydro. He began to jog, the one thing he did not want was for the local police, Jones in particular, to find him anywhere near this place.

He guessed he was past midway when he came to a gateway; there was no doubt it led to the Hydro. The fence gave way to a wall which curved in to two brick gateposts, by no means as grandiose as the front entrance he had seen in the county magazine, but in the same style — elaborate brickwork skilfully laid to appear to spiral from ground to an extreme conical stone cap.

He scanned the edges of the driveway; at each side the grass was damaged where vehicles, or a vehicle, had cut the corner short going in and out. Looking closer it was possible to see that the same tyres had made the same journey several times. So here was where the girls had been brought out, he was sure of that. But for it to have been so short a time between each trip there must surely have been another vehicle — a larger vehicle — a people carrier, or a small bus — waiting out here in the road. It seemed a feasible possibility. Even if some of the girls were willing employees, others such as Antonija certainly were not, so loading a bus, in the early hours of the morning, right outside a residential health centre would have been risky. Cannon was quite sure that while some men knew exactly what they were paying for, other clients would be outraged to know of the added extra facilities. He recalled the pitiful words at the end of Antonija's second letter: 'no good man will want me now . . . Many times I wish for death'.

A growl of anger rolled in his throat as he moved further along the road looking for signs of larger tyres, of a bus drawn up to one side to wait. He scrutinized the whole of the back boundary again, glancing at his watch as he arrived once more at the pillared entrance. He was going to have to leave, and yet he could not get out of his mind that the answer to where these girls had been taken was there for him to see if only he could persist long enough. The trouble was, he probably had not got that long. Surely there was no place inside the grounds where these girls, these sex slaves, could be successfully hidden from a police search?

He strode across the narrow road as if to view the problem from a distance, and as he did so realized there was a footpath through the dunes and grasses almost opposite the drive — and it had been well trampled. He remembered the party of elderly folk putting on their walking boots — these coastal footpaths would of course be popular.

He walked a few steps along the path, and then some metres ahead, and to one side, he saw something in the sand. It was a shoe. Nothing remarkable about that, one often came across lost shoes, socks, frisbies, balls, buckets, spades, all manner of things. When he reached it he gave it a kick, then he bent to pick it up.

This shoe was not the kind of footwear usually worn to walk through sand-dunes. This was a high-heeled shoe, a small size, four, shiny white patent leather, with brown crocodile-like skin on the toe-cap and heel. It was kind of foreign looking; a man's shoe in such a style, Cannon would have called a correspondent's shoe. It was also not the kind of shoe a young woman would want to lose.

Examining the track more carefully he began to see it was not the only pair of high-heels that had walked over it. He walked more urgently, and another twenty metres along, just coming in sight of the sea, he found the second shoe. He held the pair in his hand and wondered if this girl had kicked off her shoes deliberately, as clues, hoping against hope someone would find them and realize where she and the others had been taken. Her actions and the discarded shoes would not have been seen in the dark.

'And all things lead to you,' he breathed addressing the sea. He walked out on to the beach. There were no footprints here, but, more telling, there were sweeping scuff marks where, across this open stretch, they had been obliterated. He followed these marks to the water's edge, and here was evidence that a substantial flat-bottomed boat had been run up on to the beach.

Cannon stood and looked along the coast in both directions, wondering where the girls might have been taken. Then he looked straight out to sea. Like a tiny blemish on an otherwise perfectly clear horizon, was the outline of a ship — and something brushed very hard past every one of those sensitive tentacles in his mind.

Instead of being taken along the coast to another location, had these women been taken on board a ship? He looked at the marks beneath his feet, they could be the marks of the kind of boat he'd seen suspended at the back of large private yachts. He tried to calculate how many hours ago the women had been taken away, and whether the ship carrying them would still be in sight. And just how many ships followed the sea routes around The Wash? What he could see might be a freighter heading for Kings Lynn, or out of Boston.

As a breeze caught his face, lifted his hair, he reflected that this same sea had seen early Pilgrim Fathers try to escape from Boston to the Netherlands as they sought a better life and religious freedom. Now it might be carrying away Stefan's sister, Antonija, and a group of women who had also sought a better life. But towards what fate were they going?

The sea could be used as a universal dumping ground. He saw again the hand of the beckoning man, the body Hoskins nearly died to recover. For a wild moment he imagined a beach strewn with the bodies of young women, then blasphemed and spat to get the taste of the idea out of his mouth. In any case, he told himself, no businessman, no man like de Garro, would waste his best assets unless absolutely forced to.

He turned to walk back, wondering how much clout Brand's newspaper would have at this particular moment. Could it trace private yachts, and who owned them? He needed to talk to the journalist.

Pondering, he nearly walked out on to the roadway straight into a couple of policemen standing near their cars, but both fortunately had their backs to him, looking up the drive. He ducked back.

Were they early? He glanced at his watch: no, it was already half past four. But one thing he knew for certain, if he was spotted, his presence here could — would — give Jones the tooth-sucking satisfaction of taking him in for questioning, and with far more justification than when he had nobbled Hoskins.

Keeping his head well below the skyline he made his way back to the beach, and headed south. When he judged he must have put a couple of miles between himself and the police cars, he looked for another path inland, a well used path preferably which should mean houses, a coastal village. He was a bit hazy about the names of the villages this far south, and he needed a name to give a taxi.

Cannon jogged inland, until he came to the roadside sign for the village of Swenton, and across from the sign the village pub, the Ring of Bells. He found his local taxi firm on his phone menu and made his request. 'Be nearly three quarters of an hour, Mr Cannon,' the girl at the other end of the phone told him, 'Bill's just finishing his school run, and I'm afraid the others are on airport jobs.'

'OK,' he said, 'I'll be in the pub then, if it's open.'

'Oh, it will be,' she told him, 'they have a happy hour from 5.30.' She paused to laugh, then added, 'My chap comes from Swenton.'

'Small world,' he said.

His hand was forward to push the bar-door when someone opened it from inside. A middle-aged man in a red anorak and brown cord cap, smiled, nodded to him, stepped back and held the door open for him. 'Thanks,' Cannon said.

Inside Cannon was relieved to find he did not know the man behind the bar — that could have been difficult.

'Evening,' the landlord greeted him, 'nice evening for a walk.'

'It is,' Cannon agreed, and took his pint of lager to the window seat.

10

Cannon was picking up litter from the front of his pub — lingering, waiting for Brand — when a man in a red anorak and brown cord cap came from the car park to the front door.

'Ah! Knew I'd seen you somewhere before,' he greeted Cannon. 'You walked into the Ring of Bells last night, held the door for you.'

He was hardly able to deny it. 'I didn't recognize you, sorry.'

'I've only been here once before, passing through like now. One of many faces to you, but we all remember the man behind the bar, don't we,' he paused, laughed, and once more held a bar door open. 'You coming this way?' he asked.

Cannon shook his head. 'Bit more tidying up to do,' he said. He hoped the man, whoever he was, was not going to start talking to all his early morning trade about seeing him at Swenton. An anorak, in a red anorak. Cannon judged he looked the type to lean back on the counter and proclaim to anyone who'd listen. He had plenty on his mind already.

Brand had phoned twice, the first time had

been late the night before from his Boston hotel, to say he had lodged Stefan at Sea End, a tiny hamlet north of The Wash, with a retired journalist who passed his time picking up facts from the national dailies, adding local colour, then selling them on to local newspapers and small business presses. He was definitely up for a little extra money and a bit of added excitement.

When Cannon had been doubtful, had expected something more sophisticated, perhaps more organized from head office, Brand had reassured him. 'He's sound. Not only is he willing,' and Cannon recognized the real reason, when Brand added, 'Nick worked as a cub-reporter under him,'

But Brand *had* used his newspaper contacts and sources that morning and had phoned to say that de Garro not only owned a private yacht, but had an interest in a Norwegian cruise company. The Buckansonn Line comprised four ships based in Oslo, all accounted for; two in the Baltic, one on a Norwegian coastal voyage, one in Bergen, but the yacht had so far not been traced.

'This man is big business,' Brand had emphasized, 'tell you more when I see you.'

So Cannon was watching and waiting. He had now cleared every crisp packet, every minute scrap of paper from around the flower-tubs. Moving to the picnic tables on the side lawns he found the remains of a large take away meal, not bought at his pub. There was everything from forks to foil dishes, carrier bags and a plastic sauce container, from which ran a sticky red liquid. Scooping them up, and stuffing them into his black plastic sack, he tried to get some scale back to his anger, telling himself he could not possibly hate litter-louts as much as exploitive sex-selling businessmen. He realized his teeth hurt he had them clenched so hard, it took an act of will to relax his jaws.

He pushed his tongue to a small gap, evidence of another time when his patience had run out. He, the Cockney barrow-boy's son, had been plagued on a daily basis by a large jeering shopkeeper's lad, until the day he had taken him on. Cannon had received two black eyes and lost one of his second teeth. His mother had been appalled, but he had been unrepentant. He had felt his father silently approved, and though he could remember no visible damage to the other lad he never tormented Cannon again.

Cannon was assembling a list of relief-giving expletives in his head to help with the waiting, when he saw Brand's Mercedes. Brand must have seen him at the same moment, for he stopped short of the car park, pulled in alongside the picnic tables and got out.

'Short of staff?' Brand greeted with the air of a man who, unlike Cannon, had an immediate mission.

Cannon pulled off his rubber gloves, grinned ruefully, then demanded 'So?'

'So, I'm booked in at ye Health Hydro.' Brand sat down on a bench, leaning back on the table, 'but it was interesting. When I first rang there was some discussion as to whether they had re-opened for 'outside' bookings.'

'I would have thought all bookings were from outside,' Cannon mused, sitting down beside him, 'unless . . . '

'A favoured circle, for special treatments?' Brand suggested, 'and when I innocently inquired if they had been closed, the girl hesitated then said yes they had,' he affected a girl's superior tones ' "but only for a tiny time, for special cleaning before our busy pre-Christmas sessions." '

'Very special cleaning,' Cannon said, 'so do the reception staff have any idea what goes on?'

'All health centres have paid-up club members, this could be a very exclusive section, platinum card membership.'

Cannon growled his agreement and thought what a hard-bitten, cynical pair they were.

'How will you handle it?' he asked.

'Tip the underdog staff heavily as soon as I arrive, a trick I learnt years ago; it secures good service and loosens tongues, and I'm a past master at being 'lost' in prohibited areas.'

'And de Garro's yacht?' Cannon queried, 'do you . . . '

'*The Virgin Queen*,' Brand supplied.

'Shit!' Cannon exclaimed as if the name was a personal insult.

'Quite,' Brand agreed, 'but think of all those girls, if they are aboard, they're going to take some supervising.'

'Plus the fact that they'll be earning nothing.'

'So we're saying?'

'That we think de Garro will bring those girls ashore, as soon as ever he feels the pressure's off,' Cannon concluded.

'We need to know where that damn yacht is. My lot are working on it, but so far . . . '

'It's almost certain they'll be brought back at night,' Cannon said, 'and most likely to the same place they were taken off. The footpath from the beach comes out opposite the back entrance.'

'Yes, you said, and that's just what I think,' Brand agreed, 'and it'll be soon.'

'I'll get up there tonight and keep watch in those dunes,' Cannon said, 'and every night until they're brought back.'

'*And* once they're back, we'll spring the trap. My editor's ready to do that. A copy of my lead article about Nick will be faxed to the police, and they'll stir once they read it, believe me,' Brand said with an air of triumph. As an afterthought he asked, 'and Liz?'

'She won't be best pleased,' Cannon admitted, taking a derogatory kick at his rubbish sack now he had a more appealing mission, 'but she'll be with me all the way.'

'Yes,' Brand said, 'yes, I can see that. You're a lucky man.' He rose and held out his hand, 'I want to be booked in well before dinner.'

Cannon too stood up, and took his hand, shaking, confirming the contract they had made.

'I shall feel a lot happier knowing you're nearby,' Brand said. 'We'll keep in touch by text and as soon as my lot locate that yacht I'll let you know. OK.'

Cannon nodded and watched him go, with the conviction that actually these media people really did think they were a law unto themselves, and in his head he heard Liz say, 'yes, and they are not the only ones'. He snatched up his sack of rubbish and made his way around into the stable yard, where for the time being he had sited his waste-skips, and they might as well stay there, he thought, for all the progress the building work was making.

He lingered, reluctant to go inside, to start work behind the bar, serving, being patient, being tactful! Usually he enjoyed his customers, felt endeared to many of his regulars, but this evening would be a struggle, and at the end of it he had to tell Liz he was off out for the night, perhaps for a night or two.

He should go in, he could hear cars arriving, Hoskins's bike was already in place, and then there was the red anorak man. He muttered under his breath and nearly bumped into Hoskins as he walked hurriedly into the yard.

'What's this!' he exclaimed, 'not your going home time.'

Hoskins did not reply, but put his hand on Cannon's chest to stay him in his tracks. 'It's you who shouldn't go home,' he said, 'that Inspector Jones has just arrived, with Sergeant Maddern and another constable. They're looking for you. Maddern looks uncomfortable with it all, and I heard Jones tell Liz that . . . ' he paused, frowned, looking as if he hoped he had the next bit right, 'he said, that the face packs taken from here have the same properties as that found in the nostrils and mouth of the dead man, and they

162

found nothing at that health place,' he paused significantly. 'They've come for you, mark my words, I've seen the look on that Inspector's face before.'

Cannon stood stock-still absorbing the facts, adding up the evidence Jones might list against him. He'd found Nick's body, cut his fingers leaving his blood all over the fishing-line used as a garrotte, been seen in the Stump's Shadow in Boston — and now Liz's face-pack matched the mud on the dead man's face. 'Liz?' he queried, 'they're not — '

'He's come for you,' Hoskins repeated. 'He's gonna take you in.'

'No,' Cannon said involuntarily, and glancing at Hoskins, saw a face haunted by memories of his own incarceration, and a determination it should not happen to John Cannon.

'You'll 'ave to make a run for it then, now!' Hoskins emphasized. 'Take the footpath along the old forty foot drain, when you reach Three Brothers Rocks cut across the marsh, straight to my cottage, you can see the chimney. You'll get your feet wet, but keep straight and it's firm enough to take you.'

Cannon stared at the old poacher holding out his house key, thought of being on the wrong side of a table, the wrong side of the law, facing Jones, knowing his time in custody, his questioning, might well be much longer than Hoskins's had been, and he had Brand relying on him. He could not afford to lose the time. He imagined the frustration, and if Jones sucked his teeth, he'd need considerable self-control not to help them down the Inspector's throat.

'Right,' Cannon decided taking the key, 'thanks.'

'And I'll tell Liz somehow,' Hoskins said, stepping back outside the stable arch. He looked both ways, then gestured Cannon urgently on his way.

At a crouching run he turned sharp right, and was, in no more than thirty seconds, across the road and behind the few screening bushes along the drain. They were low and did not grow far from where the drain passed under a road-bridge on its way to the sea, but far enough for him to be out of immediate sight of The Trap.

He ran on, his thoughts with Liz. She would cope; they had run close to the wind before and survived, but his hand went to his pocket to check the comforting presence of his mobile, as soon as she was able she would phone him, he was sure of that.

He was comfortable enough running alongside the dyke, though it was an overcast evening and would be dark early. It was when he could see The Three Brothers Rocks, so called because of their elongated smooth, phallic, outlines, sunk out on the marsh, he began to have misgivings. Hoskins was certainly right, he was going to get his feet wet. He hoped it was only his feet.

He set off and realized that while the surface was thick and green with sphagnum, the immediate underlying ground beneath the bog moss, was not solid. However, as Hoskins had said, it bore his weight, though at each step his shoes were nearly submerged. His bar shoes would never be the same again, and he would be glad to be off this place. Marshes had airs, miasmas, ghosts of known or unknown victims. There were many stories of The Fens, probably retold from generation to generation to frighten venturesome children.

Cannon realised he had better take as good a line as possible on the small and distant chimney pot he could now see. He aligned it directly between two growths of reeds, taller than surrounding grasses, and regretted the lack of his compass always kept in his joggers.

He ran on, until he came to a place where there was no green covering at all, only a peaty dark morass, more black than brown. He stopped short. Was he running straight? Had he diverged from the line? He would not have thought so, but this in front of him looked completely impassable, madness to venture anywhere near, while either side the way was green-covered like the way he had already taken. Hoskins had known these marshes ever since he was a boy, but had he forgotten to tell him that he should make a divergence around this particular area? As he hesitated, a bubble rose, grew, broke with a soft squelch, and there was no way he could bring himself to start off across this bare, oozing stretch.

He had one foot poised to keep to the greener way, when a bird, a large bird, a buzzard, came screeching overhead, so low that Cannon ducked. It had a rabbit, still struggling, in its claws, a large rabbit, bringing the bird down, but the bird was reluctant to let go of its prey. An inept young buzzard Cannon thought, one abandoned the previous spring and still not practised in all the skills of hunting for itself. At the last minute it dropped the struggling creature some ten metres in front of him. Startled and awed at seeing such a bird and its prey at close quarters, he was even more astonished as the rabbit just disappeared. The green covering he had been about to commit to, opened up and took the creature into its depths, the front paws still struggling for life, it was swallowed in a second. The buzzard still tried to retrieve its meal, and Cannon found himself waving his arms to shoo it away as it nearly suffered the same fate, only the power of its great wings, a spreading, flapping flurry of black, white and brown, enabling it to pull its claws from the sucking mud. It flew away screaming it's anger and disappointment. Cannon thanked God for his own deliverance.

Shaken and rapt as he had been by the incident, he looked back the way he had come, and forward on the line he had taken on Hoskins's chimney. He gingerly put one foot into the bare morass. His shoe sank, but not above the ankle. How much did he trust Hoskins? He realized he did trust him quite a lot, even more now.

He took a deep breath and began to run on his toes, as fast and as lightly as he could, more an attempt at ballet than an out and out sprint. But the line was right, and on his toes, even his shoes did not completely disappear, there was a solid enough base to hold him. He was out of breath and shaky, not with running, but with anticipation of the worst by the time he reached the far side, and the meadow leading to Hoskins's back garden.

There was a gate through to the cottage, which he knew well enough — a couple of years ago he had searched the whole place when Hoskins had gone missing.

The old boy's vegetable garden was a masterpiece of flourishing winter vegetables, neat rows of parsnips, leeks, cabbages and to one side, smooth mounds of earth with evidence of straw beneath, suggesting potatoes and carrots clamped in the traditional manner. Hoskins, with the profits from his poaching activities, really did live off the land.

Slipping his shoes off he fitted the key into the back door and remembered that until the last time there had been excitement in the area, Hoskins had never locked his doors day or night.

Little else had changed. The cottage still had the air of a woman's touch having been long gone, of a man living alone who did his best, but that did not include refinements. Cannon reflected it must be a bit like living in an army camp, and now he was here he was at a loss what to do. At home he could at least have waited and worked. Here, well, he looked around, there was nothing that obviously needed doing. He walked through to the sitting-room — the same terribly faded pink rose cretonne on the easy chairs. One chair was very worn, the other obviously never used except as a receptacle for the morning newspapers brought home every night from The Trap, which Cannon had of course read.

The things Cannon did vividly recall were the brass-framed photographs on the mantelpiece, and as before the frames shone army fashion, but then he realized the photos inside them were not the same as before. Where there had once been a wedding photograph of a young Alan Hoskins in army uniform with his bride on his arm, there was now a photograph of a mother with a little girl, two or three years of age. It was with some sense of shock that Cannon remembered talk in the bar about Hoskins losing both his wife and his daughter in a street accident in Lynn. Billy Brompton had been telling them that a car had tried to overtake, struck another car, swerved and mounted the pavement. Mrs Hoskins had thrown herself in front of their child in the pushchair, but both had died in hospital. At that moment Hoskins had come into the bar and nothing more had ever been said on the subject.

The old man had been on his own a long, long, time, had forged a life from the little he had left. Cannon touched his forehead in salute to the man in the other shiny brass frame, Alan in Sunday best, a photograph Liz had taken last Christmas at a private dinner party they had given at The Trap for a few special friends. Cannon was moved that Alan had framed the print, and wondered at the rigours of a loneliness he had never known in his own life, and hoped he never would.

His phone vibrated. He wrenched it from his pocket so sharply he only saved it after a double juggle. Even though it was much too early for Liz to have had space and time to ring, he was disappointed to see the number was not hers.

'Just thought I'd let you know I'm booked in, just having a smoke strolling around the grounds,' Brand said and when there was no immediate response, asked, 'Are you all right?'

Cannon told him where he was and why.

'For God's sake just stay out of their hands,' he urged, 'I need you available.'

'I'll need a vehicle to be there tonight,' Cannon said, 'and they could put a watch on my pub.'

'Can you hire one? My paper'll pay,' Brand asked, then added urgently, 'Listen,' his voice dropped and it sounded as if he was walking further out into the gardens, 'the layout of this place does not add up. It seems much bigger on the outside, than it is inside.'

'How come?' Cannon asked.

'I've paced — ' he began then broke off and Cannon could hear other voices. 'I'll get back to you,' Brand said and the phone went dead.

He wondered how safe Brand was, playing a double role in such an environment.

He rang the local garage, who regularly looked after his vehicles. 'My men have gone home, Mr Cannon, is it urgent you have it tonight?' the proprietor sounded weary.

'It is,' Cannon told him.

'Nothing wrong with your jeep, or . . . '

'No,' Cannon had cut in, 'this is just a one-off.'

'OK. But as I'll have to call one of my men back in to drive a second car to take me home again, that'll cost me.'

'I understand that of course, but I'd be obliged.' There was some vigorous throat-clearing and reluctant sounds at the other end, and before the man had time to change his mind, Cannon asked, 'You know where Alan Hoskins lives?'

'Oh aye, out in the wilds. That where you are?' The man sounded almost indignant, and certainly more resigned than pleased to being obliging a regular customer. 'It could be some time,' he added.

'Fine,' Cannon made his voice very businesslike and rang off quickly.

After that he fretted around, re-ran the sound of the voices in the background to Brand's telephone call a score of times. Had the tones been threatening? Urgent? Had he heard dogs? He pondered what both Brand and Stefan had said. If there was a part of the place kept separate, walled off inside, the door Stefan had seen the girls brought out of, must surely connect to the girls' quarters somehow. So if one could gain entry through that door . . .

Then where was de Garro's yacht? He drew a map of the coast of Lincolnshire and Norfolk in the space left for doodling next to the *Eastern Daily Press*'s crossword. The great head of Norfolk beneath the deep square cut of The Wash, as if taken out by some god with three slices of a great spade. He added the deep inland clefts marking exits to the sea of the rivers: the Great Ouse, the Nene, the Welland, and above the Frampton Marshes the River Witham, named the Haven once past Boston and The Pilgrim Fathers' Memorial. He added the Hydro and the fishing lakes on the opposite side of The Wash, and filled the sea with a series of question marks.

More practically he washed his shoes under an outside tap, by which time the warning bell for last drinks should have been sounded at his pub, the towels should be on the pumps, a symbolic gesture these days, and the butt of good natured jokes — but licensees and customers knew where they

172

stood. Cannon allowed no exceptions, Paul was inclined to, if not watched, some knew and tried it on. Was tonight's closing time going smoothly, was anyone hanging on? Surely not Hoskins!

He forced his feet into his wet shoes and once his eyes had adjusted a little to the moonless gloom, felt his way along the cottage wall to the front, where he would be able to see Hoskins's cycle lamp pin-pricking the darkness as he rode home, it was beginning to be time he was here.

Cannon began to feel like an anxious, even angry, parent waiting for a tardy teenager. 'For goodness' sake,' he muttered, then started as his phone vibrated in his pocket.

In the dark he extracted it with some care. 'Liz. All right?'

'You?' she asked back.

'Did Hoskins tell you where I am?'

'He hardly had to, I saw him sidle out when he overheard Jones.'

'So what did you tell Jones?' he asked.

'I told him you had talked about having something special to do, but hadn't said what,' she paused. 'John, there was a man in the bar when Jones arrived. He listened in quite blatantly,' her voice rose indignantly as she added, 'even moved nearer so he didn't miss anything. When he heard that Jones was looking for you, he piped up with the information that you had been outside when he arrived, and seemed to be all over the place — he had seen you in the Ring of Bells at Swenton the day before. Jones was agog.'

'That's not helped my case,' Cannon said, but as Liz was agreeing he was distracted. 'I can see Hoskins's cycle lamp, he'll be here in a few minutes.'

'Jones included this interfering little man — '

'In a red anorak,' Cannon supplied.

'Yes,' Liz confirmed, 'in the general 'request' that the police were to be told as soon as ever you put in an appearance.'

'He'll have a wanted poster up next,' Cannon said.

'Yes,' she agreed flatly, making it clear she saw not the slightest room for humour. 'Paul keeps reminding me he's willing to help anytime, but wants to know *nothing* of what you are doing, 'what he doesn't know he can't tell'.'

Cannon watched Hoskins's light fast becoming a wavering beam. 'Liz,' he said, 'I won't be back tonight,' and told her of his pact with Brand.

'John, this can't go on for long,' she said quietly. 'I went outside with Jones when he left. He nodded up to our names above the door, and said we were going to have to be

174

very careful or we'll lose our licence.'

'The bastard,' Cannon retorted, but felt a pang of real unease. 'I won't let that happen,' he said as Hoskins saw him and dismounted with a sliding scrunch of boot on gravel.

Over bread, cheese, and pickled onions, which came to the table in a huge commercial-sized jar, but were homemade, crisp and delicious, Cannon told him of the ordered hire car and of his mission.

Hoskins solemnly digested the story and his supper, then poked a questioning fork at the drawing on the newspaper.

'De Garro's yacht,' he explained, 'I was trying to figure where it might be.'

Hoskins shrugged. 'Shouldn't be difficult,' he said. 'It'll be logged.'

'How logged?' Cannon wanted to know, 'and who by?'

'No mystery about that,' Hoskins said. 'Ships do log each other when sighted, keeps a record of last movements should anything happen, important part of seamanship.'

'You been to sea then?' Cannon asked.

Hoskins shook his head. 'Know plenty who've spent their lives on the North Sea or in the local docks.'

'So if de Garro wants to take these girls back very soon, where do you think he would order his yacht to go?'

'Well if he wanted to put in somewhere, then Lynn of course,' he said. 'King's Lynn.'

'Lynn?' Cannon remembered newspaper pictures of an enormous freighter off-loading steel reinforcing bars. 'I thought it was all commercial stuff,' Cannon said.

'Mostly . . . yes, but they have the odd naval vessel, that Dutch sail training vessel came in not long ago, and he'd only have to say he thought he had engine trouble and they'd fetch him in with a pilot boat. I reckon they'd let that man's yacht in, no problem, but I could find out for you tomorrow,' he nodded towards the old-fashioned black telephone which stood partly obscured just beyond the draining board.

'Any chance tonight?' Cannon was asking when they both heard the sound of cars stopping outside. 'My hire car,' he said.

11

It had not been the three men walking in the grounds that had surprised Brand when he rang off from Cannon, or the fact that two of them were in brown security uniforms, it was that each of these two held four leashes each, on the end of each leash a huge Alsatian. The third man spoke; he was undersized, had on a dark well-worn suit, and his face was so deeply pock-marked as to look almost distorted.

'It's all right, sir,' he called, 'they're just being walked before they go into their pen for the night.'

'Quite a hustle,' Brand called, deliberately going nearer, testing while they were restrained just how aggressive these animals were. All the dogs gave voice as he stepped nearer, but made no effort to pull towards him. Neither the behaviour of the dogs, nor of the men, felt quite right to him. Guard dogs, he believed, were trained not to bark, and each dog had its own particular handler, they weren't walked in packs, but he found the third man far more sinister, and felt a shudder run down his own broad back as this man approached him, with what he assumed, was a smile on his face.

'You've good security here,' he said, nodding towards the two men as they led the dogs away.

'Not lost are you, sir, this late in the evening, out of sight of the house?' the smiling man asked.

'No, no,' Brand assured him and indicated a path in the opposite direction to the dogs. 'Just a short stroll after dinner. Goodnight to you,' he added, walking away.

He soon realized that inevitably all the paths this side of the Hydro would lead to the fishing complex, and he had other matters on his mind, he turned back and found the man still there.

'I thought I'd wait and walk you back to the house, sir,' he said. His smile conjured up images of old war films, of prison camps and sadistic punishments. 'Your first visit?' he asked falling closely in step, too close for Brand's comfort.

The conversation they had was multi-layered, banal on the surface, with probes that might be innocent inquiries or piercing investigation. Brand wondered if they had both learned that each was not quite what they seemed. The man, to his relief, did not enter the conservatory with him, but wished him goodnight, an enjoyable stay and walked rapidly away, turning his face away from the lights. Brand wondered what job he filled here. He could not help his face, but he was hardly someone de Garro would want on show at a health spa.

He took the lift up to his third floor room, anxious now to phone Cannon again, realizing it was quite a comfort to know the ex-Met man would be nearby during the night. He intended to have a stiff drink from the room's mini bar while he talked to him.

'Watch it!' Brand exclaimed as, following the room-number signs, he collided violently with a man coming the other way.

'Sorry, sir.' The man, who was taller, swarthier and heftier than Brand, had on a short white waiter's jacket which was not quite large enough. He looked as if he had just delivered a meal, for a covered tray stood on a butler's stand, outside the door next to Brand's room.

'Take your time, man,' Brand said. 'What's the rush?'

'Orders, sir,' he said, and went to move on.

'Just a minute,' Brand said, 'is this your corridor?'

The man clearly did not understand what he meant.

'Do you look after these rooms?' Brand

gestured along the corridor, held up his room key and pointed to his allotted room.

A look almost of panic crossed the man's face. 'No, no, sir,' he said and with a movement like a boxer avoiding an uppercut, he swung round Brand, and was away, not quite at a run, but at a fast lumbering walk. Brand asked himself if all the staff was odd. The majority were certainly Slovaks or Portuguese — he supposed a good country-man would employ his own if he could, though they all seemed to have their own agenda. He began to feel the people who were in the way were the ordinary customers. Though he reflected he could feel that in his local superstore.

The service in the dining room had been adequate but monosyllabic. His steak had been superb, but it seemed the full menu was not available. He had observed this being explained to other diners who appeared to be outside members with family and friends celebrating birthdays and anniversaries, not residents. Just when he needed to find someone who would talk to him, no one wanted to. Except Cannon he reminded himself, he would certainly be wondering why he rang off so suddenly.

He let himself into his room, where his bed had been turned down. He looked around to see if anything else had been disturbed, putting his hand into his right jacket pocket for his phone, and then the left, then going to his inside pockets, then more wildly his trouser pockets. The certainty grew that it had been lifted.

The pockmarked man had walked uncomfortably close, if he was a practised pick pocket the snatch would have been easy, and he looked like he knew every trick in the criminal trade. Then he had been barged into by a waiter with an ill-fitting coat.

In his car he had a new phone he had picked up for Stefan, as well as other aids-to-the trade, all locked in the boot. He decided as well as needing the phone, he also needed to know more about the layout of this place. Two birds with one stone then.

He took a miniature brandy from the mini bar, had a swig and put the bottle in his pocket. He was going to learn nothing stuck in his room. He'd been writing up stories for years, the one he would tell reception as he handed in his key was that he was going to see an old friend, and would be quite late back. But first a little exploring.

He left the room as noiselessly as he could, noting that the covered tray was still outside the room next to his. On an impulse he paused to lift the napkin. There was no food, just cups without saucers and a jug which did not match. He replaced the napkin. The deceit riled as he walked silently along the red-carpeted corridor, not following the signs to the lifts, but diverting to a corridor which announced no room numbers and where the carpet was deep blue, though just as luxurious. The other main difference was there were no lights on in this section, though he could soon make out the white sign with large black letters on the door at the end. It announced: 'Private Quarters'. He listened at the door then tried it: it was locked.

He went back, realizing that this blue corridor ran towards the rear of the building, while the red corridors, where the guest rooms were, probably all ran across the length — he had seen only red carpeting as he had come up in the lift. An idea occurred to him: he went back past his room to the far end, which looked as if it terminated in a blank wall relieved by pot palms. He nearly turned back, but past experiences of things not being what they at first seemed, made him want to go and push his hand at the wall, confirm it existed.

Pushing a hand through the all screening greenery he found nothing. Above his head was an archway which, with the palms, gave the impression of a blank wall, but he found that again there was a left turn towards the back of the building, blue carpeted.

Looking down he could see where the huge pot at one end had at some time been moved across the carpet. He squeezed through. Some twenty metres in the carpet stopped; under his feet the gritty feel of raw concrete. It was now more passage than corridor, and passing his hands over the walls, there were certainly no rooms off it. He began to feel almost claustrophobic. He'd heard of a deafening silence, this was it: the space seemed to close in around him.

He needed a light, yet even if he found a switch he would hardly dare use it — but he did have a rechargeable torch in his car. Perhaps it was the thought of going back that saved him, perhaps he had kept his weight on his back leg, for as he stretched forward there was nothing to support his outstretched foot. Just in time he threw himself backwards. He went down heavily enough to knock the breath from his lungs, and do his coccyx no good at all, but as he explored with his feet from where he sat, he realized it could have been worse. He was on the edge of certainly more than four or five steps, which was as far as he could stretch his legs down, and it could be a whole flight, and at floor level there was a smell of — he grimaced in distaste

— animals, or a whiff of drains?

It seemed like a good time to go back to his other idea, for the time being at least. He edged backwards before getting to his feet, and once in the bright lights of the lift he brushed himself down, carefully stretched his back a few times, then shrugged and circled his shoulders. He had to appear relaxed.

'Going out, sir?' There was an elderly woman in reception, Portuguese like de Garro, her black hair so lacquered it looked like an enamelled wig. 'It is late to be going out,' she added.

'Seeing an old friend,' he said breezily, 'I'll probably be quite late, night porter will be on I assume.'

'Of course, sir, no problem there,' she said, but she held his eye almost as if challenging him to back down and stay put.

He glanced away from her prying black eyes to a list of treatments the spa offered. He picked it up, saw that the bottom third had been covered by a plain strip inside the frame.

'Do I have to book for any of these?' he asked, and before she had a chance to answer added, 'I was hoping to have some of those Black Sea mud treatments I occasionally have in London, I enjoy them. Do you not do them?'

It threw her, her mouth opened and closed a few times, and while she was nodding affirmation, her lips formed the words, 'Not at the moment, sir.'

'Not at the moment?' he repeated.

'We . . . we . . . ' she cleared her throat, 'we had trouble with our supplier, so I am sorry at this time, no.'

'Oh, disappointing,' he said making a show of pouting and shaking his head.

'Well,' she began rallying, 'we were not supposed to be open for residents for another day or two, things are . . . not in place . . . '

'After refurbishment,' he suggested.

'That's right, sir,' she said relieved for his help.

'So are the permanent staff away?' he asked. 'You know, the ones who give the treatments? I know I spoke to a young English girl when I booked in.'

She looked at him so sharply her hair bobbed, but all of a piece. 'A few are on holiday, yes sir.

'Never mind,' he said, thinking he had pushed her far enough. He treated her to his most charming smile and said 'there's plenty more I can chose from. See you tomorrow then, goodnight.'

'Goodnight,' she said, and only remembered the 'sir' as he was walking away.

It hadn't really ruffled her hair, it would take a gale or two to do that, but her composure, yes, though whether that had been wise was another matter.

He went straight to the car boot for the new phone, but, leaning for a moment on the back of his car, he knew something was amiss, for it gave a faint click as if he had not properly closed it. He suppressed the urge to open it immediately, sure that somewhere he was being watched via the closed circuit cameras perched high above the car park. He opened the driver's door as if he suspected nothing and drove out, turning in the direction Cannon would come.

When he was well clear of the spa and sure he was not being followed, he stopped and checked: the boot was empty. He was thankful he had left his laptop in his room in Boston, but wondered what they would make of the collapsible ladder and the matting. The only bit of kit they had left him was the rechargeable torch in the glove compartment.

He needed a phone, but he needed to see Cannon more. He settled down to watch and wait, hoping that Cannon would spot his Mercedes. Another thing he liked about Cannon, apart from his loyalty to friends — and to justice — was his love of old classic cars and that old Willy jeep!

There was not much in the way of traffic; just three cars came towards him in the next three quarters of an hour, then after the headlights of a small sedate saloon had passed over his car, it stopped and reversed, and he saw it was Cannon at the wheel.

'Couldn't you get anything better than that?' he asked as Cannon joined him in the Merc.

'Lucky to get anything,' Cannon said, 'and I nearly drove by. What're you doing out here? I was worried when you didn't phone back, I thought I heard dogs.'

Brand told his story, and in the silence when he finished, the Fen night seemed darker, grimmer, as if it could hold any threat the two of them could imagine. 'Probably not wise for you to go back,' Cannon said.

'Wise?' Brand laughed. 'I'm on the brink of the biggest story of my career, and I'd do it for Nick even I wasn't. I'm going back down that bloody blue corridor and those stairs tonight,' he was saying as Cannon's phone gave its ring tone, which sounded like a bullet reaching its target. 'Christ,' he said, 'that's enough to give you palpitations.'

'Hello, Alan, yes . . . '

Brand could hear Hoskins shouting at the other end. He caught odd words which made him more than curious.

Refolding his phone Cannon told him, 'De Garro's yacht was logged in The Wash by several freighters now in Boston Harbour.

'So she's not docked?'

Cannon shook his head.

'There's a jittery air at that Hydro — and with the staff — like being at that bloody Bates Hotel in Psycho,' Brand said.

'The *Virgin Queen* could be sailing back as we speak.'

'So back to our original plan,' Brand decided leaning forward to start the car.

'Just a minute!' Cannon exclaimed. 'We've one mobile phone between us, and as I see it, you might need it more than me.'

'So who would I phone, if not you?'

'I think Hoskins in the first place,' Cannon decided, 'he's canny, he knows the whole situation. I'll put his number in at speed dial one for you,' which he began to do as he talked, 'and I'll speak to him again now, say that if you're in trouble you'll phone him, and he's to alert Liz.'

'Liz?' Brand queried, 'wouldn't she be better first?'

'She's too concerned, she'll ask too many questions if it's you or me,' he said, 'but she won't argue with Hoskins, she'll just use her judgment, as in raising hell and every policeman in the area to get to us pronto.'

'OK, but we don't want this springing too soon,' Brand agreed and once more reached forward to the ignition. 'An empty trap achieves nothing.' Once more Cannon caught his arm before getting out of the car.

'You do know you could finish up like Nick. De Garro is . . . ' memories of the flayed fish chose the description, ' . . . a ruthless, satanic, murderer.'

'And what a privilege it'll be if we can nail him,' Brand said and turned the key. ' "Satanic", good word, I'll quote you.' He tossed his arm in an airy salute as he swung the car back towards the spa.

12

Hoskins had found him a torch, a waterproof coat and a filthy woolly hat. Cannon was glad of them all as he tried to relocate his way to the path through the dunes.

It all seemed so much further in the dark, with nothing but the tiny light, a memory of the boundary fence, and, when he came to the back road, the grass verge to guide him. Eventually he came to the place. He turned on to the sandy track and moved on steadily, thinking of Brand inside surrounded by de Garro's dogs and strange staff. He was glad to be in the open air, even though his feet in his wet shoes were icy-cold, and the squelchy sand made his feet wetter and colder with each step. He stopped. He should surely not be on wet sand. The path to the edge of the beach should be dry, not this cloying, soaking stuff he was dragging himself through. He had wandered off the track, or more likely he had strayed on to another track diverging from the first. He took another couple of steps and felt the clinging dampness of his shoes and socks loosen as his shoes filled with water.

He backed up a few steps, cautiously raised his torch higher. Not only was he in water, he was at the edge of a small inlet and no more than a few meters in front of him was a boat, a small boat with a portable outboard engine. It looked so familiar but he had to be sure what he was suspected was true, and paddled in. If it was the boat Hoskins had discovered, the same one he thought belonged to his rival poacher — to Ivo Levak, the man whose body they had pulled from the sea, now drawn in near the Hydro — there might be quite a few things of interest for the forensic people here. With water up to his knees he had hold of the boat's wooden side; he shone his light around inside, checked the make of the outboard, a new Suzuki, he'd remember that. It would be a pleasure to let Jones know he had found the boat again.

He turned to go back, and as his face caught the breeze from the ocean, he realized there were lights, moving pinpoints out at sea. He swore with gentle satisfaction, if this was the *Virgin Queen* already coming in, Hoskins's informant and their own calculations had been right.

He hurried now, surprised how far he had strayed in the dark, but when he arrived at the original track, he understood why. The path he had wanted diverged a few metres

191

around a large dune, while the track he had followed in the dark had seemed straight ahead.

He reached the beach and the lights out at sea seemed nearer, and stationary. How he wished he could contact Brand, who was probably even at that moment, exploring his blue corridor and staircase to lower regions of the spa. He turned to look inland and from the direction of the Hydro a light flashed three times, Cannon swung back towards the sea in time to see the answering three lights from the boat.

The cover of the dunes petered out at the beach and from the sea he heard the sound of an engine being started. He had not much time, and it was possible men might come from the Hydro to meet the returnees. He made his way back to the steep dune where the track split, and scrambled up, using the clumps of marram grass as hand and foot holds. By the time he reached the top he judged he was at least a metre above any man's head. He lay flat, still, and listened. He could hear the engine of a boat coming inshore, and was in no doubt they intended to land at much the same spot they had embarked from.

Above him the moon made a late and fitful appearance, swathed in cloud, but visible. He shot a message to the sky: not now, not now! From the direction of the house came voices — he wished for an entrenching tool as he tried to get lower behind the stiff grasses he could now see outlined against the paler sky. He silently urged the men to get on with their task before it became any lighter.

Soon he heard feet swishing quickly across the sand and when they were below him, he heard one man say, 'No, you fool, this way,' before relapsing into Portuguese, and there were more questions and brief answers in the same language from two more men, so four going down to meet the boat Cannon calculated.

It was not long he knew, though it felt far too long, before the heard the men coming back, the same men and a group of women who were urged along with fierce menaces. The men only had need of a whip to be proper slave-drivers, Cannon thought.

This group was followed by another party, about the same size he judged, two men this time, he thought, who must have come with perhaps five or six women, from the yacht.

'Shall we have to make another journey?' a young man with a local accent asked.

'Not sure,' a deeper, older, voice answered.

'I don't like it,' the young man said.

'I'd keep that to yourself I were you,' the

older advised, 'but I know one of the chaps from the place is coming up with that odd lot.'

'They're not tied together like the others,' the first man stated.

'No,' the older man gave a short ironic laugh. 'They're drugged up, that's why. He'll manage them if he can keep 'em on their feet. Then there's one more group, and that's it.'

The slave-train picture was complete in Cannon's mind, and he wanted to rear up like some terrible revenging monster, instead he clenched his fists and swore he would get them all. He'd often pondered the question whether any true Englishman, and by that he knew he probably meant a true Cockney, would, if ordered, carry out say, some of the atrocities and violations inflicted on the Jews during the Second World War. What he was witnessing now, was a man caught up in something he obviously did not relish — Cannon had seen it many times in his Met days; young men caught up in activities, gangs, they wanted no part of, but were too afraid to leave — and there had always been a big bad villain, a posturing bully, a bogey man, like de Garro, they were afraid of. Bringing such men down had been, was, Cannon's mission.

So he mustered what patience he had and

waited for the next party, the drugged group, and wondered about the 'long parcels' Stefan had seen being loaded into the van. Had these been troublesome ones knocked out with drugs, carried out in blankets?

This party seemed a very long time coming, but then he heard a very different sound, a sweeping, shuffling noise of people barely able to drag their feet through the sand. This, then, was 'the odd lot', and as they passed beneath him and beyond his hiding place he raised his head. At the same moment two other things happened, the moon came fully out from its cloud for a brief second and the last woman well behind the other two looked back and up, as if straight at him. He had seen that face before; he had seen her in a flowered cotton frock with frills, her hair tidily rolled into a halo all around her head, her face as full of life and health then, as now it looked vacant, pallid, unawares. As he watched the first woman of this lot stumble and fall, the man ran forward, kicking at her, wrenching her to her feet, trying to make her go on.

Cloud closed over the moon and Cannon remembered his promise to Stefan to save his sister. Activated by the kicking and the opportunity, he slid down the far side of the dune, grabbed Antonija, put his hand over her mouth and pulled her bodily to the far side of the sandhill, holding her unresisting body tight against his chest.

He, John Cannon, was mad, he thought, as he stood stifling any sound Antonija might make and holding his own breath, as he heard the final group of women and their captors coming up from the beach. They caught up with the man trying to get the fallen woman up. He heard the anger, the fear of delay, in the men's voices, as they urged him to 'lift her', 'carry 'er', then a furious, 'get 'er other arm.'

Listening as if his life lay on it, and it probably did, Cannon heard the two groups move off together, without it, seemed, having missed one of their charges.

Without sparing thoughts of how long this reprieve would last, Cannon lifted the girl bodily, and carried her along the path towards the inlet. She gave no resistance, was limp in his arms.

When he reached the sea, he paddled out and laid her gently in the bottom of the boat. She threw out an arm as the boat tipped, he caught and folded it gently into her side, whispered her brother's name, 'Stefan,' he said, 'Stefan, Stefan, your brother, has come.' She was still and he felt she was listening, listening like a young child, or an animal, in the depths of distress catching a word they knew.

Cannon wondered how much worse he had made matters, as he climbed in next to her. He had an illegal immigrant in a boat, a drugged illegal immigrant in a boat probably used by a murdered man, and a hire car in a distant solitary lay by.

He wondered what his chances were of getting Antonija back to the car, even if she was able to stagger some of the way, which seemed doubtful, for she lay so still and as the sky began to lighten with the first hint of dawn he could see her eyes were open, wide, still, staring. Had she not shrank back a little as he took off Hoskins's coat and placed it over her, he might have thought her dead.

The boat, he decided, had to be the better option. He waited until he thought the men must have gone back to the yacht, wondered about the outboard engine, but felt to start it might be inviting trouble. All he knew was he had to make a move, get this girl away before full daylight. He dare not wait any longer.

He pulled the oars from the bottom of the boat and was trying to fit them into the rowlocks, and his legs around the girl, without disturbing her, when she spoke. 'Stefan,' she whispered.

'Yes, yes,' he said, 'Stefan. I am his friend.'

197

To his surprise she slowly took herself to the stern of the boat out of his way, giving him the feeling she knew about small boats — perhaps there had been a lake near her home. He helped her with the coat, and she pulled it over herself. Cannon took one of the oars and pushed down into the sand to ease them out into clear water and into the first signs of real dawn. Soon he was out deep enough to row properly. He had fixed on what he must do: he would row along to the beach with paths leading to the village he had found before, to Swenton; from there if Antonija was recovering they should be able to walk to the hire car and be away before all but the earliest workers and risers were about.

He rowed with long smooth strokes, grateful that either the curve of the coast, or the fact that the *Virgin Queen* was already underway, meant the yacht was out of sight. He knew he had never been so cold in all his life; his feet and legs felt like blocks of ice and any warmth the rowing raised seemed to turn immediately to cold water on his back, but they were soon in sight of the beach he wanted. Shorter by water, he thought, a phrase often used by an old Thames waterman, a friend of his gran.

He pulled into shore, jumped into the

water again and hauled the boat up. He held out a hand.

'Stefan's friend,' she said.

He repeated her words, adding, 'I am taking you to another friend. A safe house, and soon you will see Stefan.'

She nodded and made an effort to climb from the boat, but she was very unsteady; she would never be able to walk far. He helped her up the beach and wondered if he could convey the idea of giving her a piggyback. He said the words, but she shook her head. He made gestures from her to his back, then crouched down and indicated his back again, but she staggered backwards instead of in his direction. She was much weaker, or more drugged, or both, than he realized. Before she had time to recover her balance, he stooped down in front of her and lifted her up over his shoulder in a fireman's lift. 'Keep still,' he said, 'or I shall drop you. I have a car a little way away.'

It became a little easier once he had left the beach and the sandy track for the tarmac of the car park and its approach road. Seeing the sign for Swenton over to his left he could have wished it was opening time at the Ring of Bells. He put Antonija down when he reached the road proper, held her hand gently, kept contact, helped her keep her balance, and took a breath. When he had recovered sufficiently he looked at her more closely now the light was better. She was so pale compared with the photograph he had seen of her, and her eyes were wide and staring, the pupils dilated. Her image had been fresh and unspoilt, the reality — he looked away.

He had one last effort to make; he put his arm around her waist to support her and they walked and rested, walked and rested, and reached the car. Antonija gave a great gasp of disbelief as she was seated in the passenger's seat. 'Stefan?' she asked.

Cannon was so exhausted that as he nodded he hit his head on the steering wheel and let it stay there for a full minute. As he started the car he thought of the man he was leaving at the spa and wondered if Brand had already rung Hoskins.

To his surprise, as he helped Antonija from the car and up Hoskins's path, the front door was pulled open, a rare event.

'This is Stefan's sister, Antonija,' he said. 'Has Brand rung?'

'No,' Hoskins said, and nodding to the girl, added, 'Is it, now,' before he led the way inside, his lack of words soon made up for by his practical attentions. He swept the newspapers from the spare armchair, ushered her into it and pulled an ancient crocheted chair cover from his own chair and put it over her. Then he put the kettle on, and came back from the kitchen carrying a hessian shopping bag, which he handed to Cannon. 'Kept meaning to bring these back,' he said. 'You'd best put them on.' It was his old track suit Liz had found for Hoskins after they had recovered Ivo's body. Hoskins added a pair of socks and a pair of slippers, and holding all these Cannon nodded towards the phone, 'OK?' he asked and picked up the receiver. Glancing at his watch he saw it was 6.30 and realized Hoskins had not only kept watch but had kept his coal fire going all night. They were glad of it now.

He dialled, the old phone seeming to take an eternity to circle round and back to ring the long mobile number. Then there was a long enough pause for him to accept the hot sweet tea Hoskins had made and have several grateful sips as the number was picked up and rang out. There was no answer.

Was it possible Brand could just be asleep, sound asleep? He rang off, did not allow himself to dwell on random speculations. He dialled the pub number. Liz answered almost immediately, the relief in her voice as she heard his voice brought a tear pain from eye to nose bridge, he turned away from Hoskins and the girl who were watching him intently.

'Thank God,' she said, 'since Hoskins rang the once, I've heard nothing.'

'I need — ' he began, but what he needed was legion, and he heard himself say, 'I've got Stefan's sister — '

'Antonija? Where?'

'With me at Alan's cottage, but . . . ' he did not say that he needed clothes, shoes, or that mostly he needed to see her, a kind of touching base thing to feel right, instead he asked, 'Is it safe for me to come home?'

She seemed to hesitate for a moment, before saying 'Yes.'

'You're sure, no one hanging around? I can't afford to be taken into custody by that clown Jones, particularly not now.'

Again there was a hesitation, then once more, and more heartily, she reassured him. Had it not been Liz, had he not trusted her, had she not been his life, he might have questioned further. 'See you in a few minutes.'

'Are you borrowing Alan's bike? I thought you didn't — '

'Hire car,' he supplied and rang off. Now he had the difficult task of making Antonija understand she must stay with Hoskins, but she had watched the old man as he had looked after them, this, plus the fire, the tea and now a bowl of cereal with warm milk Hoskins gave her, she seemed ready to stay, to rest.

'Keep her here,' he said to Hoskins as he left.

'I shall do my best,' he said. 'She looks as if she could sleep. I'll put hot water bottles — ' and he stopped there and looked as if that might be a daunting task.

'All right? You all right?' Cannon asked.

He nodded, 'Yes,' he said, 'I've a bed I've kept aired and changed for over forty years, time it was used.'

13

Driving back to The Trap in the pale light of a chilly dawn Cannon felt uneasy. There had been a kind of holding back, a kind of 'I've bumped the jeep' tone in Liz's voice that gave him pause, that seemed to need a face-to-face confession, perhaps she would throw her arms around him first. He wouldn't object.

Pulling into his pub car park he saw there was a car there, but not one he recognized. It could of course have been left by a sensible drinker who had over-indulged the night before. It did happen. Cannon encouraged it with a notice above his bar, with the simple message: 'Your car can stay the night.' They had planned to add 'and so can you' to the taxi-hire cards pinned there by punters, when the stable conversions were finished. All on hold, he thought wearily.

As he walked towards the kitchen door, it opened, and Liz come out and stood tall, pale like the dawn, her long blonde hair falling loose around her shoulders and as beautiful as a goddess to Cannon. He hurried to her.

She met him two steps from the door and they embraced for long silent moments.

Whatever she had done, if anything, he knew he would always forgive her.

'John,' she said, 'Paul's here.'

He pushed her to arm's length, so he could see her face. 'You sent for him?' he asked.

'No, it wasn't like that, you'd better come inside,' she said, adding, 'Helen's with him.'

His hands dropped from her shoulders. 'You mean he's here with Chief Inspector Moore,' he stated.

Another slim tall woman, dark haired, in a pale green woollen dress was on the doorstep, watching, listening. 'Liz didn't ask me to come, John,' she told him, 'it was my decision. Inspector Jones reported you were away from home, no one was saying where, and Paul's been roaming around all night. So putting the two together and making . . . ' she shrugged the probable answer to that, turned and led the way inside.

The 'all night' was not lost on Cannon, and as they reached the kitchen Paul rose from the table, looked him up and down, paused at the frayed check slippers. 'Natty!' he said, and pulled out a chair for Cannon, adding, 'before you fall over by the look of you.'

'So, time for frankness,' Helen invited his co-operation, prompting, 'John?'

In the silence Cannon heard the central heating click on, and the tiny noises as the heat began its journey through the pipes and radiators around the pub.

'Well, we have more information,' Helen told him as he hesitated. 'Liz told Inspector Jones that the London friend you had gone out with was staying at a Boston hotel. Jones has been busy, found the hotel, the room. This man, Keith Brand, appears to be a journalist working on the *Daily Endeavour*, and according to the material found with and on his laptop — ' she caught the accusation of powers overstepped in Cannon's eyes, she frowned, defied him to say anything and carried on, 'The employment agency letters given to Archie Burns, your builder, this national newspaper concocted — forged. Jones has not yet managed to contact Brand.' She had watched Cannon closely as she spoke, 'But you already know all this,' she added.

Cannon put his elbows on the table and his head in his hands, staring down, needing to hide his thoughts, his indecision, from this chief inspector, authoritative even in her pale green dress.

'Helen's on your side, John,' Paul stated, 'only *she* can't say that.'

Cannon knew that was probably true, raised his head, decision made, and met Helen's eyes directly. 'Brand is at the Health

Hydro,' he said and told of Brand's connection with Nick and Stefan, and his peril. 'There's obviously different staff, and it seems to me that it was a mistake Brand's booking being accepted.'

'Risking his life for a story,' Helen condemned.

'And for Nick,' Cannon heard himself add, 'then there's the immigrant women — '

'Listen, John,' the chief inspector went on, 'Maddern has uncovered a string of people, regular houses, where girls working illegally as au pairs and general domestics are kept on low pay, real economic prisoners, then they seem to disappear. Maddern believes they are, or were, directed by the late Ivo Levak to the Hydro, when 'there's a vacancy' was the phrase used by the sergeant's informant, a Croatian shelf-filler in a local supermarket. She tried to get a job for a friend she knew was arriving, but the friend went straight into the illegal domestic market and she's never been seen or heard from since. Maddern reported she was described as a tiny pretty girl.'

There was a moment's pause as all extrapolated from that fact. Liz broke the spell by sweeping her hair up and back into working mode, secured by an elasticated red hair band from her pocket. 'A vacancy,' Liz said, 'I shouldn't think anyone is allowed to leave, it suggests a death, and so far it has been men who have been found murdered.'

Helen's voice fell to a grimmer level. 'We have had inquiries from Interpol about a spate of young women found on the beaches of southern Norway. 'They have all been naked, murdered, in various ways, and forensic scientists have found they had all suffered serious sexual attacks over a length of time. Link this with what Maddern has found . . . '

Cannon had locked into his earlier imaginings, a beach strewn with women's bodies. He had to force himself back to what was being said.

'But Norway?' Paul was puzzled, 'and, apart from that, I thought the search of the Spa here, found no evidence of anything other than a bona fide health and fitness resort.'

'Because de Garro was tipped off by his upmarket clientele,' Cannon supplied, 'and de Garro's yacht brought the women, including Stefan Tomac's sister back to the Health Hydro tonight. I was there.'

'You were there!' Helen exclaimed. 'We were not even aware he had a yacht! He doesn't seem to share that facility with his circle of friends. Is this true?'

'*The Virgin Queen*,' Cannon supplied.

'The bastard,' Paul breathed.

'He also has an interest in four cruise liners, the Buckansonn Line based in Oslo,' Cannon added.

'You'd better explain,' Helen said. 'But you are certain you saw this Stefan's sister?'

'The girl in the photo found in Stefan's jacket, yes.'

'And where did you get the information about the yacht and the cruise liners?'

'Brand's newspaper,' he answered, 'but Hoskins found out the *Virgin Queen* was sailing last night, and incidentally . . . '

The next piece of information had them all gasping out exclamations, staccato.

'You have the girl?'

'You've left her with Alan?

'Quite a bombshell, old boy.'

'I'll have to take action on this,' Helen said.

'So you'll go in again,' Cannon stated, 'quickly before anything happens to Brand — if it hasn't already. How will you work it? De Garro must not be forewarned *again*.'

'No careless talk,' Paul said.

'No,' Helen agreed, 'no talking, texting or tweeting. This man crosses many boundaries, even the highest echelons are not immune.'

Cannon shot her a startled glance, remembering that she had been on her way to see the chief constable the last time she had been at The Trap.

'The chief himself instigated the last search. He asked to see me because I am his most senior woman officer.'

'So incorruptible,' Paul interrupted.

'Well, less likely,' she said and went on: 'he had been approached by one of his superintendents whose sister is married to the Vice Chancellor of our biggest eastern university, and she had come to him really on behalf of her husband, who suspected that there was some kind of undercover sex club in the area. His staff have found there is a lottery being run among some male students, with the money all going to one prize: a very expensive visit for two to a health club that combines 'other services'. The lottery was regarded as a lark, but it's growing and becoming darker, more covert. He and his tutors are very aware of conversations that stop abruptly when they hove into view, and there was a wrongly directed email. He was sufficiently worried to send his wife as a kind of envoy to see her brother.'

'This Superintendent,' Cannon mused, 'has probably been a guest on one of de Garro's estates, shooting.'

'I don't think he shoots, but there are certainly senior officers, and senior men in our civilian departments who do, so we must be careful. But it gives me direct access to the Chief, at any time. I shall go now straight to his home. He wants face to face on this.' She reached for her coat. 'You'll stay at home, John, until you hear from me.'

It was more order than request, but he nodded.

'I'll stay here,' Paul said, 'I'm not being sidelined now.'

'I feel a bit concerned about the girl with Hoskins. He's an old man — if she decided to make a run — '

'I'll go over, take . . . ' Liz paused to think, ' . . . a few underclothes and things Hoskins certainly won't have.'

'Could we get Dr Purdy to go over and have a look at her?' Cannon asked. 'She's certainly been drugged.'

'I could do that too,' Liz volunteered, 'he'll come, he's a friend.'

'I'll get straight back to you as soon as I've seen the chief,' Helen said, 'but I think I'll request a woman PC should go over to stay with the girl and Hoskins at his cottage,' she said, 'better than having to take her to a hospital.

'Yes, good idea,' Cannon said quickly, as if giving official sanction to the idea.

Paul walked out to the car with Helen and

Liz came over to stand behind Cannon, gently massaging the base of his neck. 'John, you have to go to bed.' He groaned with exhaustion and pleasure. 'I'll drive over to Hoskins's right away,' she said, 'see they're both OK. and be straight back.'

'Wait until the WPC gets there,' he suggested, 'this is all going to come to a rapid climax. It should take no more than a few hours to reassemble enough men for a comprehensive raid.'

'Come on then, I'll see you upstairs — '

'And I'll hold the fort downstairs,' Paul said coming back and hearing the end of the conversation.

Cannon let himself be escorted upstairs, but made sure he had the phone from behind the bar with him. He waited while Liz selected underclothes, a warm jumper and trousers, then some of her toiletries, even a bar of lavender soap.

'Hoskins probably only has carbolic,' she said as she kissed him on the top of his head and instructed him to undress, 'You'll relax better.'

Once he heard her car leave he made another call to his own mobile. He waited and waited. There was not even a ring tone. Did that mean the phone had been destroyed?

He had made a kind of tacit vow with Brand that neither of them would rest until de Garro was brought to justice — and he'd made a verbal promise to the journalist.

He pulled out the diary he had transferred from his own suit. He kept much information in this diary, using it much as he had done his official police notebook. He found the number Brand had given him to alert the *Daily Endeavour* that the story was about to 'break'. He had a code word so that the man at the other end, who he obviously roused from sleep, would know he was genuine. The word was Eastabrook which he understood was Nick's real surname.

'That's not Brand?' the man asked.

'No,' he replied.

'John Cannon then.'

'Yes.

'Can you get back to me with any specific times?'

'I'll try.'

'Right.'

He made one more call to the home of the retired journalist where Stefan was in safe keeping. 'Tell him his sister is safe,' he said.

The man's answer was brisk and to the point. 'Give me the postcode where she is, I'll drive him to see her,' the voice was authoritative. 'I've heard his story. It's the least I can do before the poor bastard gets interned, or something stupid.'

Before falling back on the bed in clothes and slippers, Cannon reflected he probably really had started something, put up a few hares. What he prayed it would turn out to be was the beginning of the end for Vasco de Garro. This was his mind's last grip on waking facts and he fell asleep mixing the villain with one Vasco da Gama, who had done some sailing and . . . was Portugese, wasn't he . . . ?

14

As the lift doors opened, the woman Brand had last seen behind the reception desk looked very startled, her hand flying to her mouth, fluttering to her throat and the neck of her frilled blouse.

'You are back earlier than — ' she broke off.

'Than you expected,' he supplied, then added, 'me too. Friend not well,' the lie came without pause, and as she left the lift and he entered, he caught her odour of perspiration and stale make-up. He reached towards the lift buttons inclining his head graciously as he did so. 'Goodnight to you, madame,' he said, thinking she looked as uneasy as he was once more beginning to feel.

She scurried to her place behind the desk, from which he had helped himself to his key, which had still lain where he had placed it. She was reaching for the phone when she looked up to realize he was still watching her. Her hand fell to the desk, landing on a ledger, which she flipped open but did not consult. Brand pressed the button and the lift doors closed, whoever the woman was he was convinced she was not a receptionist, and she was certainly about to report his return to someone.

The corridors to his room were deserted; he had the feeling he could be the only resident staying over. Even if that were so, and breakfast time tomorrow morning should prove or disprove that theory, there was certainly an atmosphere, what the *Daily Endeavour*'s theatre critic would call a 'brooding silence'.

He reached his door, looked back, listened, and went on. The sooner he solved the mystery of the blue corridors and stairs the better, so once more he walked to the end of the red carpet, to where the potted palms obscured the left turn to the unlit corridor.

He felt well equipped this time with mobile phone and the rechargeable torch. On the far side of the greenery he went cautiously on until he reached the end of the carpeting. Here he stopped, took the torch from his pocket, and shone it downwards.

The end of the blue carpet had been professionally finished with a gripper-rod. On his right was a door, with a Yale lock, but no knob or handle on his side. He pushed his fingernails into the crack, but it was locked. Swinging the light higher he realized a wall had been knocked through at the point the carpet ended. A metal girder spanned the gap above his head and the walls beyond had been panelled with what looked like hardboard. Shining the light directly forward, this wooden tunnel went on as far as the beam carried.

He walked on, aware of a faint crunching beneath his feet, it sounded like a thin layer of sand on the concrete surface. He had not noticed this the first time he'd come this far.

He came abruptly to the stairs. If there was any suggestion of recent work in the materials of the panelled passage it ended here. This flight of downward steps was part of the original structure and each brick tread was hollowed in the centre by many generations of menials. A way had been knocked through from the old main house to the servants' quarters, and as he walked downwards he could imagine many a burden of coal, water, laundry, and everything else it took to service the gentry of the old house, had been manhandled from basements to above stairs and back.

He came to a flat stone-flagged passage, quite short, no panelling here, the walls had been white, or lime-washed, at some time. He reached the second flight of steps down, and the fetid smell he had noticed when he had fallen on his first visit was becoming worse,

217

he took his handkerchief from his pocket and held it over his mouth or he felt he would gag, choke, give his presence away, if there was anyone near enough to hear.

His room was three floors up so he had expected there to be three flights down, but he paused at the top of the third flight. There was a cloying sense of dampness, he shivered, the sense of claustrophobia was almost overwhelming. He was not a man who suffered from such sensations normally, but as he began this descent he felt he was going into the bowels of the earth — and it smelt like someone's bowels, he thought, and there was a slight film of something slippery on these steps.

He kept the beam of light under his feet and he saw his shoes left marks, where there had been none before. If no one else had been down here for a time, was there anything more worth exploring? It was only a momentary thought, he had come this far, he would see all there was. Clasping his handkerchief tighter over his nose and holding the torch with the other, he felt the need for some support and put one shoulder against the wall to steady himself. It was a mistake, for leaning he slipped, though not far, and he regained his balance two steps down. He didn't even make much noise, but from below came a howling and a barking, like the Hound of the Baskervilles times ten, with echoes. The din was shocking, appalling, but he knew now what the stench was seeping up these stairs: The dogs — those supposed guard dogs — were kennelled somewhere down here, without much ventilation. But why, for God's sake?

He had automatically switched off his torch and now turned to retreat, to feel his way back. Then above the baying and barking he heard a man shouting for the animals to be quiet.

'Were they fighting?' an angry man demanded.

A muttered defensive denial. 'They're all right.'

'So why're they barking? Get in there, see if there's anyone in the cellar or up these stairs.'

'No one comes all the way down.'

'I had a message from the desk, go and check.'

So his return *had* been reported, Brand began to climb upwards as fast as he dare, heart pounding. He heard a door being pulled open below, then, as he reached the landing between the third and second flights, he heard a noise from above. It was the sound of a heavy man lowering his weight from step to step, a small protest of air coming from his lips on each drop.

Brand had nowhere to hide, only a choice between at least two men and a lot of dogs and a single heavy man coming down. He slipped his torch into his pocket and forgot about secrecy, springing up the stairs to challenge the descending man. He caught him by surprise some six steps up. Brand charged, wrapped his arms around the man's legs in a tackle any rugby player would have been proud of, and threw him sideways at the wall. A flashlight flew from the man's hand, hit the wall and floor with a clatter and went out, but Brand had already recognized the hefty waiter in the tight white coat.

The man swore and as he fell tried to grab and hold on to Brand, but Brand was past him, above him, able to push him off with a thrust of his foot, and run on, up the second flight of stairs. A different kind of mayhem broke out behind him now, for as the men below shouted up to the waiter, the dogs began to bark again.

Brand's first instinct was to escape, to run, to quit the hotel, reach his car and be away. But, ever the chancer, the optimist, he rethought his plans as he scurried upward: last stairs; concrete floor; carpeted passage, and through the palms. By the time he had come out on to the red corridor he had decided that if it all became heavy, there was no way he was going to admit to being anything other than a punter looking for rumoured extra services, and if he got away with that, it could eventually *add* to his news story.

He reached his own room, hesitated outside, the corridor was empty, quiet as the grave — he wished he hadn't thought that. Did he go into his room, phone Hoskins, or did he try to reach his car? Logically if he was sticking with the punter story then it made sense to go into his room, even though he knew the wrestler-type waiter must have recognized him. Common sense told him to run, to risk there being just the elderly receptionist with the lacquered hair on reception. There was no way she could stop him escaping. As he lingered those vital seconds he heard the whirl of the lift's approach and then the swish of its doors. He was disconcerted to see de Garro himself approaching him, the man's width seeming to completely block the corridor. Then behind him he heard pots and plants go flying as the waiter and two other men burst through.

The only temporary way out was his room, but as he fumbled for his entrance card the door of his room swung very slowly open. Inside was the undersized man with the pockmarked face and the worn suit. He beckoned Brand inside with a revolver.

De Garro followed, nodded in the scowling waiter, and then with a dismissive nod to the other two said, 'Get rid of his car.'

15

Cannon woke to the knowledge that his feet were unbearably hot. He struggled to rise from where he lay crossways on their bed, groaned as he saw Hoskins's plaid slippers and thick grey socks. It was broad daylight. He looked at his watch: one o'clock — lunchtime! Where was Liz? What was happening downstairs? What was happening at the cottage and the Hydro? Brand?

He pulled the slippers, socks and tracksuit off, went to their bathroom and had a cursory wash, looked at his stubble — it matched his black-rimmed eyes — threw fresh clothes on and ran downstairs. There were voices in the bar, the smell of bacon, and as he entered the kitchen Polly, Helen's spaniel came to greet him as Paul rushed through from the bar.

'All right, old boy?' he asked. 'You don't mind Polly, couldn't leave her on her own.'

'Of course not,' Cannon fondled the dog's long ears, asking, 'But what's happening?'

'Haven't heard a dickie-bird from anyone. The womenfolk just said wait to hear, and I've obeyed orders.'

'No Liz?'

'Presume she's still waiting for the woman PC to turn up.'

Cannon paused, listening to the voices from the bar. 'You've opened,' he stated.

'Not the first time,' Paul said, 'it was easier than have them knocking at the door. Done a few all-day breakfasts too,' he said. 'Want something?'

Cannon shook his head. 'So no news from Headquarters either?'

Paul shook his head. 'If Helen's embroiled with the hierarchy she probably hasn't had time to do much else. They'll be organizing another swift raid on your Hydro I imagine.'

The thought of it being his Hydro made Cannon shudder. 'I'll go over to Hoskins's place,' he said. 'You all right here?'

Paul nodded, 'But let me know what's to do, old boy.'

Cannon nodded. 'Will do.'

The seat of the hire car was soaked, so he took his jeep. Ten minutes later he was outside Hoskins's home and parking behind an ancient Rover and Liz's red MG. No police vehicles he noted, and the Rover, well it had the air of a retired journalist about it. He put a hand on the bonnet — the engine was still hot.

Inside he found Hoskins, Liz and a man he judged to be in his early seventies, tall, lean, tanned, a shock of grey hair. He stood up as Cannon entered.

'John, this is William Bose — Nick and Keith were both reporters when he was news editor on the *Daily Endeavour*.' She too stood up as she added, 'William, this is my partner, John Cannon.'

William nodded and smiled, he had a charming slow smile which made Cannon think of retirement on 'Golden Pond' and he noticed Bose had a mole high on his left cheekbone — it would have been a beauty spot on a woman.

'You've brought Stefan?' Cannon asked.

William nodded. 'He's with his sister. We thought we would give them a little time on their own. I've only just arrived.'

'He won't even have had a cup of tea,' Hoskins said to no one in particular and moved off into the kitchen.

'And I know you've only just woken up,' Liz said looking at John.

'Yes, I expected you'd be home quite quickly.'

'So did I, but they've had two domestics and a teenage girl incident, so I said I didn't mind waiting until there was a woman PC available.'

'So you have heard from,' he was about to say Helen, but changed it to 'Chief Inspector Moore.'

225

'Yes, like you two,' she included Bose in this, 'they're concerned about Brand, and they're trying to secure the whole area around the Hydro without alerting anyone,' Liz said.

'Bring the net in slowly so no fish escape,' William Bose said, looking directly at Cannon, who immediately knew this man was aware he had contacted the newspaper.

'Are they tracking that yacht and covering the beach?' Cannon wanted to know.

'They'll be using the latest satellite tracking system to cover the shipping in the area,' Bose said, making Cannon wonder if he meant the police or the newspaper.

At that moment the door opened and Stefan came in with his arm around his sister, who was hugging a book to her chest. 'We heard you come, Mr Cannon,' he said. He allowed himself to be drawn forward, still supporting his sister, until she reached Cannon, then still clutching what Cannon could see was a very old Rupert annual in one hand, she grasped Cannon's hand with the other. She bowed her head and kissed his hand, saying over and over, 'Thank you, thank you, thank you,' and he felt her tears falling on to his hand.

Cannon stooped to try to look at her face, but she tucked her chin deeper into Liz' s mauve polo-necked jumper.

'She is happy, and ashamed,' Stefan said as he too grasped Cannon's hands. 'I am always in your debt,' he added. 'Always.'

'She has nothing to be ashamed of,' Cannon assured them both as Hoskins came in carrying an old tin tray full of mugs of tea.

'Nothing,' Hoskins echoed.

Antonija now pulled her hands free and went to Hoskins, held out the 1970s Rupert annual towards him and said something in her own language.

'Antonija says we had such books when she was a little girl, and that you are her second father,' Stefan translated, and now it was Hoskins's turn to drop his eyes as he scowled confusion and fussed with the tea.

'Sit down, m'dear, sit down,' he ushered her to a chair with a brimming mug, but as he would have moved away she caught his hand and held it tight. She sat with the precious Rupert annual on her knee, making Cannon wonder if the annuals had been translated, or whether Croatian children just followed the stories from the illustrations. Hoskins seemed pleased his daughter's book, as well as her bed, was of use again, and gestured urgently with his free hand for Liz to hand round the other teas.

Bose moved a dining chair so that Hoskins

227

could sit down next to Antonija, and Liz handed him a cup of tea. Cannon thought it all looked like a stage-set, and he felt a growing compulsion to be the manager.

'Right,' he said almost before he himself was quite prepared for the next action.

'Antonija says there are young girls, very young . . . ' Stefan began but stopped when everyone looked at him with such concentrated concern.

'Whatever your sister can tell us about the place will help the police,' Cannon told him. 'They are planning another raid in the next few hours.'

'We're hoping the other girls will be rescued and the culprits caught,' Liz added.

Stefan told his sister, she responded by clenching her fists, shaking them in tiny beats of approval and speaking urgently to her brother.

'She wants to tell you about the dogs,' Stefan said, and even as he talked, his sister went on in Croatian. Soon he was nodding and translating in short gobbets of information. 'Dogs kept in cellars at back. Only girls there . . . locked in. If girls shout, dogs bark. Girls in room above dogs . . . locked in . . . and guards with guns. Girls taken to small rooms for men. If good, gain trust, taken through locked doors to better rooms, bedrooms with windows, but — ' Stefan's voice wavered and he had trouble bringing himself to translate her next remark, 'but nuisance girls taken away, not come back. No one wanted to be nuisance girl.'

Into Cannon's mind came Stefan's story of blanket-wrapped forms, the naked bodies found on the beaches of southern Norway, and finally of a man beating a hapless fish. He felt a wave of nausea sweep over him, and as Antonija raised her face, every one in that room registered the humiliations and the fears this girl had suffered.

'Can you tell us of the ways you were taken in and out of the building?' Cannon asked, feeling she must not be allowed to lapse into a silence at this vital point. 'Was there more than one way?' he prompted.

She nodded, and turned again to her brother, obviously understanding better than she could express herself, in English. Once more she began to speak but with added urgency.

'Many passages,' Stefan translated. 'When she first taken there, in van to side entrance, long way and down stairs. Then there is back way. Nuisance girls back way, through dogs, and my sister heard words of Ivo's boat. Taken out back way, through dogs, to beach, small boat to big boat. Then back and — '

Here Antonija looked up at Cannon. 'Rescued by Mr Cannon,' Stefan ended.

'You were very brave,' he said, nodding to Stefan to translate.

She shook her head. 'Afraid,' she said in English.

'Can she tell us anything more about the guards, how many?' Bose asked quietly.

The question was asked, but clearly she did not seem to have any idea, although Stefan repeated the numbers she recited, 'seven, eight, nine, ten . . . ' ending with the same shrug, and ' . . . but many more on boat.'

'They're not an issue if the yacht's sailed,' Bose said.

'The issue is to take de Garro,' Cannon began but stopped as they heard another car stop outside.

Liz was nearest the window. 'It's the doctor,' she said.

Cannon went to meet him and before they walked back into the sitting-room had answered Richard Purdy's questions and given him a quick summary of the situation.

'Sorry I couldn't get here before,' he said, 'the police have been keeping me busy ever since surgery.'

When he walked into the room and put his case on the table, Antonija sprang up, shaking her head. She held the annual like a shield,

230

edging away to stand behind Hoskins' chair.

'You said she's been given drugs,' Dr Purdy said quietly to Cannon, 'obviously injected against her will. She's not going to take kindly to me. Is she talking, making sense?'

Cannon said she was.

'And how long has she been here with you all?'

'Over eight hours.'

'Probably nearer twelve,' Hoskins said.

'Then I'll just leave some sedatives, to be used if you think necessary, otherwise, unless you think there is physical injury I judge it best to leave well alone for the time being. You can always call me again.' He took a small bottle from his case and handed it to Liz, smiled and nodded to Antonija, then everyone in the room started, except the doctor, as the telephone rang. 'One all round perhaps,' he suggested drily, then pausing to learn that the call was not for him announced he wanted to try to complete his house calls before evening surgery.

While the call was being answered by Liz, Cannon walked the doctor out through the kitchen. 'The police will undoubtedly need a full physical examination later,' Richard Purdy said, 'she's obviously been abused mentally and physically, the effects will last a long time.'

'Until the end of her days,' Cannon corrected.

When he returned it was Bose who was on the phone. 'His newspaper,' she mouthed to Cannon, and he knew then Bose was not here just to bring Stefan to see his sister, he was the newspaper's man on the spot. There was a lot of mere yeses and noes, interspersed with, 'a few hours, I'll let you know.' Bose listened for quite a time after this, eventually saying, 'This near the coast, and with a yacht involved, a helicopter I would have thought. The nearest airport?' Bose hesitated for a moment, looked questioningly at Cannon, who supplied, 'Northmarket' which Bose repeated.

'A helicopter?' Cannon queried as the receiver was replaced.

'Might be useful, don't you think?' Bose answered, adding as if in justification, 'this is a big story, Nick's epitaph in a way.'

'But hopefully not Brand's,' Cannon muttered. 'We should be hearing from — '

There was the sound of another car outside. 'Busy corner of the world today,' Bose said.

'And this is the police,' Liz added.

'Helen?' Cannon asked.

'Sergeant Maddern,' she corrected, 'and a woman in plain clothes.'

232

The sergeant and Elaine Schultka were introduced, but Maddern lost no time in pleasantries. Turning to Cannon he said, 'Chief Inspector Moore would be glad if you'd come with me to help out with one or two details.'

'Details?' Liz demanded, 'what kind of details?'

'Everything I know, I suppose,' Cannon said brusquely.

'We already have a cordon around the area. The Chief wants to move in swiftly, and John has been to the scene before,' Maddern said.

Cannon was at the door. 'And I have all the information from Stefan and her sister.'

'John!' Liz exclaimed, 'please . . . ' but she cut herself off, left whatever plea she was going to make unsaid.

'Go back to our pub,' he said, 'look after things, let Paul know what's happening.'

She did not answer, but he saw in her eyes the expression they always held when she thought he was exceeding his powers, stretching his luck too far and for a moment he wanted to rush back to her side, put his arm around her waist and say he was staying.

'These things are usually tied up fairly quickly when everything's in place,' he said instead. 'Helen's wasted no time in the organization.'

'And we must be moving,' Maddern added. 'Are you happy for the others to stay here for the time being,' Maddern asked Hoskins who sat holding Antonija's hand where it lay on his shoulder.

'Of course, they're welcome.'

'Mr Bose?' Maddern queried.

'I'll be around somewhere,' he said, adding as if it were an afterthought, 'my old newspaper is flying a helicopter up to Northmarket. You should both have my mobile number.'

'With photographers,' Maddern cut into what Bose made sound like small talk. 'You keep them well out of the way, until this operation is over.'

'Don't worry, sergeant, my greatest wish is for the guilty who've caused this misery,' he looked across at Antonija and her brother, 'and my young friend Nick's death, to be behind bars.'

Details of mobile numbers were taken. Maddern put Bose's number into his own, then turned to Cannon, 'Brand has yours I understand, but not contacted you?'

'He has not,' Cannon confirmed grimly, adding to Liz, 'I've got the bar phone.'

'OK. I've got my own,' she said.

'Right,' Maddern said, 'let's get off.'

Liz followed them out, her car keys in her hand. She raised a dutiful-looking salute to

Cannon as he climbed into Maddern's car.

Maddern glanced across at Cannon as they drove away at speed. 'I expect she knew exactly what she was getting when she teamed up with you,' he said.

'You reckon?' he asked grimly.

Maddern grunted with laughter. 'Reckon you both did.'

Cannon changed the subject. 'We're not going in the direction of the Hydro,' he said.

'No,' Maddern confirmed, 'Chief Inspector Moore has set up her headquarters in her partner's cottage. Lot of things about this case that are unconventional,' he paused to laugh again. 'Inspector Jones, who's been sent out to supervise the far side of Swenton, may have apoplexy at any moment.'

'There's always a bright side,' Cannon acknowledged.

'The general feeling is that the chief inspector sent him out of the way, so he didn't arrest you on sight,' Maddern said and, suddenly serious, added, 'and he has made a good case. Your blood all over the fishing-line when you found the first body, then you find the second. Then Liz has mud packs with the same constituents as found in the first victim's nose and mouth. The only reason he didn't rush you inside immediately on that one, was that so had Chief Inspector Moore and a woman PC, but you are, as Jones rightly says, always around.'

Cannon knew what the sergeant was saying, as he drove at some speed along the fenland lanes, was nothing but the truth.

'If you take my advice, tell the high-ups what you know, then keep out of everyone's sight.'

Cannon remained silent.

There were already several cars at the back of Paul's cottage, and ahead of them a sporty red kit-job was also just arriving. A tall well built young man unthreaded himself from the driving-seat and a middle-aged, slim woman more gracefully from the passenger's side. Without looking at the other car that had just arrived the couple went to the door, the young man reaching forward to knock, then stepping back to allow the woman to enter first.

Helen Moore, still in the pale green woollen dress waited in the doorway as she saw Maddern and Cannon had also arrived. 'Good timing, you complete the party,' she said, 'come in, let me tell you who is already here.'

She introduced him first to a giant of a man made more impressive by his police superintendent's uniform. 'This is John Cannon, sir.'

'I've heard a lot about you,' the superintendent's hand was all enveloping, his eye told of doubts shelved for the time being. 'I am pleased you agreed to join us — we obviously need a neutral civilian.' The statement was enigmatic but he did not pause, turning to introduce Cannon to the woman and young man who had just arrived. 'This is my sister, and her son, Simon,' he said.

Ah, Cannon thought, now we are getting to it. A student and member of the university lottery, no doubt, and built on the same lines as his uncle. The older man's stony expression as he looked at his nephew did not bode well for the next private encounter between the two, but this was no time for niceties and Cannon addressed Simon directly and to the point.

'I think we both know why we are here; you've been inside this Health Centre as a customer, I've explored outside, and I have information from one of the girls kept encarcerated, also,' he paused meaningfully as if daring Simon not to co-operate, 'there is a man inside in danger of losing his life. Shall I start or will you?'

The young student looked from his uncle to his mother as if he wondered what right this unshaven, unkempt, looking civilian had to begin procedures. His mother pulled out a chair from the table for him, gave way for her brother to sit next to him.

'How was your visit organized,' Helen prompted.

'My friend and I had to go into the restaurant as if for a meal,' he began, 'we were told to express a preference for a table with a blue cloth, and then we were to write on the menu that we preferred the blue dining-room. The waiter took the menu from us, bowed, went away, then came back after a few moments and said we were to follow him. He took us to the lift, I noticed he handed the menu we'd written on to a man standing near the lift.'

'What was he like?'

'He was like a thug in a pin-striped suit. I just thought . . . ' he shrugged. 'He was a kind of posh bouncer, like some of the clubs.'

'Describe where you were taken,' his uncle prompted.

'The liftman got out and the thug who now had the menu took us up three floors. We went through some rooms marked private. We seemed to go quite a way towards the back of the place, then turned right, and from then on everything was blue, the walls, the rooms. Jake,' he cut the name off quickly, as if he had not meant to say it, 'the boy who'd won the lottery for two people, I was his guest.'

The superintendent's throat clearing was more a growl than a necessity.

'Well, he was taken into one room and me into the next, and there was no knob or handle on the inside of those doors — we were prisoners really. It was a blue bedroom, with a blue bathroom, and about ten minutes later a . . . girl was delivered.'

'You were there for?' Cannon asked.

The young man looked disconcerted, his mother tutted and said, 'How long were you there?'

'We had two hours,' he said, and now any lingering air of bravado had evaporated.

'Was the girl willing?' the boy's uncle demanded, and Cannon saw Maddern, father of three daughters, clench his fists.

'I think she was afraid not to . . . ' was the answer that trailed off.

'And how did you leave?' Cannon prompted this time.

'Exactly the same way, just in reverse order. The girls were fetched away, we were left alone again for about ten minutes, then we were let out, taken back through the private quarters, down on the lift and out.'

It was Cannon's turn now to retell his own and Antonija's experiences. As he finished Simon put his head into his hands and exclaimed, 'Oh God! We didn't realize.'

'No, I hope not,' the superintendent said, 'and I have to say we took the family there for a New Year party last year and stayed overnight. The thing with this man de Garro is that he has built up a local reputation for generous gifts to charity and is lavish with his private entertaining.' He paused, then added, 'and this blue cloth and asking for the blue dining room, where we slept, the rooms and corridors were all decorated in red, red and gold in the bedrooms.'

'I remember the carpets outside the rooms where we were taken were also blue,' Simon added.

'We must make sure all the officers detailed to go into the building know this,' Helen Moore said.

'So when the police went in the first time none of this was found?' Cannon asked, glancing at Simon, who frowned and dropped his gaze to the table.

'Nothing,' Helen confirmed. 'I feel in retrospect there was a lack of real ruthlessness in our search.'

'When you went into the private quarters,' Cannon addressed Simon again, 'where was the door through to the rooms where the girls were brought to you?'

'We went into a kind of library. There was a door standing open between book shelves opposite the door we entered by.'

'A concealed door then,' Helen said. 'I went into that room — there was only one door in and out that I could see.'

'See the men also know this before they go in again,' the superintendent said.

16

He had drawn maps, racked his brains for every detail that might ensure a police cordon was sealed tight as a vacuum, and then suddenly Cannon was out of it. He had seen the steely conclusion of the session in the superintendent's eye, and the apology in Helen's, as he had been thanked and delivered back to his pub.

Showered, shaved, behind his counter, helping Liz with the evening trade, it felt unreal. Reality was somewhere closing in through the fishing complex, secreted behind picnic areas, drawing in along the beaches, through the dunes. It was a lighted fuse, fizzing its way to the explosive.

He hoped they had checked de Garro's car wasn't parked for quick escape near the fishing lodge, and that the boat, Ivo's boat, he had used to rescue Antonija had been found — that would be on Jones's patch. He could even have wished he was with Jones coming in from beyond Swenton. Watches checked, times planned, signals arranged . . .

'John,' Liz said from against his elbow, 'would you like to go and put together a large well done steak, salad and a basket of chips.'

He looked at her as if she had spoken in a foreign tongue.

'Well, you're no use in here,' she hissed at him. 'People are talking to you and you are not answering.'

'Who?' he demanded and glanced around, to find Billy Brompton and his wife, the big, Irish, red-faced, Madge, plus a couple of members of The Trap's darts team, staring at him. No one spoke and even Billy made no wisecrack, so Cannon knew he must have been acting strangely. He swept out of the bar and behind he heard Billy ask, 'What's spat him out? Acting like a bloody prima donna,' and there was a gurgle of laughter as Billy added, 'he even tossed his head.'

He imagined Billy imitating the gesture, but reaching the solitude of the kitchen, Cannon felt he had cause, even Hoskins was more involved than he was. Hoskins was at home with two of the most important witnesses, while he was . . . ? He opened the fridge, stood staring at the packs of steak, wondering just what level of disuse he had fallen to. While he stood there Liz also came through to the kitchen. He was immediately on the defensive, snatched the nearest pack of steak, closed the fridge and scowled. 'I am doing it,' he said, 'not urgent is it?'

'I'll do it,' she told him, 'there's someone here to see you.'

'Who is it?' Cannon wanted to know.

'I've no idea, I don't remember ever seeing him before.'

'Did he give a name?'

She shook her head.

'Police? Another newspaper man?'

'John, I *don't know*, go and see while I do the steak. Take him upstairs, he looks like a man who'd rather be anywhere than here. Billy'll give me a call if anyone wants serving. He and Madge are sharing the steak and chips.'

'This pub is getting like a Fred Karno's outfit, a do-it-yourself emporium.'

'I wonder whose fault that is,' she stated.

The newcomer in the bar was conspicuous if only because every eye was on the small stocky man who had turned his back on the curious customers and was concentrating on where the landlady had gone. John came as far as the counter flap, felt his mood change in a second as he immediately recognized the man. There were not many people Cannon had had an exchange with, particularly an unpleasant exchange, who he did not instantly recognize again.

'Come through,' he said, and did as Liz had bid, took him upstairs to their sitting

244

room, and gestured him to a chair, with the words, 'This is quite a surprise.'

'You remember me?' the man asked.

'I would have to look at your card to recall your name,' Cannon told him, but keeping his voice light, without recrimination, he added, 'I tend to remember window cleaners who nearly shut my hand in their van door.'

'Pavao Mekish, sorry, I . . . ,' he said, but there was none of the pride, or the arrogance, Cannon remembered in the man, who having introduced himself, now seemed unable to continue.

'I am wondering why you've found me, and how,' Cannon asked, aware his own ego was returning as he watched this man go to pieces. He went to the sideboard, poured a small brandy and offered it to Mekish.

'How? I pulled in behind some bushes after . . . we met . . . watched you go by. Garage men know Willy jeep, owner of pub who used to be in the Met.'

Cannon felt a growing sense of excitement, though he knew even if this little window-cleaner was going to admit posting Antonija's letter, it was hardly vital evidence now, but Mekish looked as if he had much more on his mind.

'I think you are guessing something I come to say, but,' he leaned forward, clasping his

245

hands between his knees and staring down at them, 'not all.'

'You did post the letter you found with money on a windowsill,' Cannon stated.

The man nodded. 'I knew I should not touch it, that the big man — '

'de Garro,' Cannon said, wanting no doubts, but immediately wished he had not, for Mekish doubled over, holding the brandy in his two hands but forehead resting on the glass. He was visibly shaking, obviously completely traumatized.

'What on earth has happened?' Cannon asked. 'This is about more than the letter you posted?'

Mekish slowly sat up again. 'I would not have touched it, but the address, I knew the place in Croatia, near Porec, my parents came from there, I . . . ' he let out his breath in a great sigh. 'I have been terrified ever since I took it, then when you stopped and asked me about it, I thought you were one of de Garro's spies.'

'Spies?' The word surprised Cannon.

'Many of us could not make a living here without him — we work in his pub, his clubs, on his land — but we're afraid. He is a violent man and some are paid to report on others,' he paused, his bottom lip trembling like a child about to burst into tears, just managing, 'some disappear' before having to grit his teeth to regain control.

'Someone close to you?' Cannon asked.

Mekish clamped his teeth tighter for a second or two, then drew in a deep breath. 'My best friend. He is jolly, tells jokes, full of talk, we go to the races together always, Newmarket, and — '

Full of talk, Cannon did not have much doubt who that might be. 'Ivo Levak,' he suggested.

Mekish dropped his head in assent. 'I try to turn blind eye to many things, but now I think he is going to escape all he has done. We hide how much we hate him, his gold rings, his power, his money made . . . ' his English, though good, now failed him.

'Exploiting others,' Cannon finished for him, gesturing him to take more brandy, thinking that through man's history much good had been done by sudden small whims, like posting a letter, but greater evil by not doing and questioning things, sensed and seen to be wrong.

The brandy gone, Mekish took a deep breath. 'I clean sections of the Health Spa every week,' he began. 'This morning was the turn of the side offices and staffrooms. I always go early, as soon as it's light to do this old part, I like to be out of the way before the staff and others, big man's aunt,' he paused to shudder, 'she lives there, are about. There are small balconies outside some of the rooms, the aunt's, the big man's office. Today I was really early, too early. It was difficult to dry the windows off, makes it hard work. I was on his office balcony, when I realised he — '

'De Garro?' Cannon poured him a smidgin more brandy.

'Yes, had come into his office. I heard a noise and looked in but he was busy. There was a small suitcase on his desk, and he had opened a safe that stands in the corner, he was taking things out, little boxes fell on the floor, like jewellery boxes He was just . . . ' he described the action with a great scoop of both arms, 'in great hurry to empty safe.'

Cannon sat down slowly, anxious not to distract Mekish now he was getting to the crux of his story.

'I was terrified he might see me. My ladder was at one end of the balcony, so unless he came to the window, but . . . ' he swallowed with difficulty. 'Then I heard a knock at big man's door. I think he closed his safe and case before he called 'come in'. I recognized the other voice; it was his right hand man, terrible face,' he made pecking motions with his fingers at his own face, 'terrible man, they call him the Vulture behind his back, he's

248

ugly, and always watching. He tells big man he has dealt with the car, but not sure what to do with man.'

Cannon's heart lurched with the certainty that this would be Brand.

'Big man say he has to be dealt with quickly, and what about the boat. Vulture says they cannot get out to sea far enough, everything washes back in with tides and couldn't he be kept until . . . ' Mekish paused to shrug, 'there are girls to go abroad.'

The implication of the remark might have been lost on Mekish, but Cannon thought of the naked bodies found on the Norwegian side of the North Sea.

'Big man furious, says he should have got rid of the man and the car together. He has a business meeting in London, Vulture must deal with the man, and he wants it all tidied up before he comes back.' Mekish shook his head, 'I do not believe, you do not take contents of safe to business meeting, and I think someone else is going to die.' He pushed himself back in his chair and Cannon could imagine how he must have flattened himself against the balcony wall as de Garro talked to his headman.

'I think he is running away, leaving other to — '

'Carry the can.'

Mekish nodded. 'I think his game is up, and it has something to do with this man and his car, and,' he paused and though his voice trembled, he stated, 'and I do not want Senhor de Garro to get away.'

'Nor me,' Cannon endorsed.

'But . . . to go to police . . . I have been in this country a long time, but — ' Mekish paused, 'then I remember you stopping me, asking questions, and that you used to be a policeman, you would know what to do.'

'But you say this all happened early this morning.'

'Yes,' he confessed, 'I was delayed, and it was not easy to come here.'

Cannon wanted to say that it wouldn't have been easy for the man the Vulture had to dispose of either. He found himself wondering if Brand was still alive. He was fairly certain it would not be possible to reach Chief Inspector Moore or anyone else at that moment; the operation would be well underway. He would have to go, force his way through. 'Finish your story,' he said.

'Vulture goes, then big man, office is empty and the case gone. I climb down from balcony, decide I will leave at once, and never come back, there are windows to clean everywhere. I am at the side of the building and I see big man leave in his car, driving very fast out of the drive.'

'Did you see, or hear, which way he turned?'

'No, I could not see end of drive, then the aunt calls. She is on her balcony shouting that I have not cleaned her windows. She keeps asking me why I was carrying my ladder away when I had not finished. I say I do not wish to disturb her. She waves me back, then she watches me finish all the work. She says she will not have people wandering about, instead of doing their work, and I had better do a good job or she will tell Mr de Garro when he arrives. So she does not know he has already been, emptied his safe and gone on 'business meeting in London'.'

'What time did you leave the spa?'

'Nearly midday.'

It seemed clear that unless de Garro was already in custody he had left before the police cordon was fully in place. But had they found Brand?

Cannon rose asking as he went to the door: 'So it's taken you all afternoon to come here?'

'Yes,' Mekish said. 'The police stopped me, but I said I was coming here to clean your windows.'

Cannon could see he could waste time getting himself into a question and answer session that would get him nowhere but it would certainly not help Brand. 'Will you be going back to the address on your card?' he asked, 'Will I be able to reach you there?'

Mekish nodded, somewhat reluctantly, then asked, 'Could I come and clean your windows, so if the police ask . . . '

'Yes OK.'

'I tell you how much when I've looked round,' he said.

Cannon frowned, said nothing, wondered if he had expected the man to do the job for nothing. He should have known better, and was slightly annoyed with himself as he offered the man yet another drink when they reached the bar and he accepted it.

'I have to go to see Helen,' he said to Liz, 'alright if I take the MG, I'll be quicker.'

She was in the middle of serving Mekish and Cannon was away before she could do more than nod reluctantly and look alarmed.

As he drove, well beyond the speed limit, towards the spa he pondered what Brand might have told de Garro, if anything. Then he wondered if he should get in touch with Bose, or the number Brand had given him. He stopped the car abruptly — once with the police he might not have opportunity to make these calls. He called the number Brand had given him, gave the code word and said the time was 'now'. Bose he advised to stand by

252

near the helicopter, and rang off — he had no wish to debate the point, it just felt right.

Though he saw nothing as he passed the entrance to the fishing complex, once he came in sight of the front drive of the spa he felt he had never seen so many people on a raid before. There was a fleet of ambulances, a range of police vehicles as if displaying the variety on offer, and a melee of people around the front porch, but it was the white van slewed half on the drive and half on a flower bed that held his attention. He parked and began to walk towards it. This was undoubtedly the van Stefan had described as being the one the girls had been loaded into and unloaded from at the side door of the Spa. It had a long scratch all down the driver's door.

A policeman in body armour and helmet began to move towards him, shouting for him to stand still, not to touch anything, but the constable was in turn hailed by Sergeant Maddern, who came quickly over to Cannon.

'I have to see CI Moore urgently,' Cannon said. 'Is she here?'

'They're all here,' Maddern nodded towards the house.

'The van in the flowerbed?' he asked as they walked towards the front entrance.

'It jumped the road-block and was driven

253

in just after we arrived, and were concentrating on the house.'

'The driver?'

'We've got him. The men at the road block thought there could have been two men in the van, but we've not found anyone else,' Maddern shook his head, 'and the driver hasn't said much up to now. He's obviously terrified of his boss.'

'Have you found Brand?'

'They're still searching. This place is like the Crystal Maze.'

'But you've found the women,' Cannon noted as several were escorted out of the side entrance swathed in blankets and helped into one of the waiting ambulances.

'Locked in two rooms, like animals,' the sergeant answered, adding, 'and there's another thing you might like to know. The place where Stefan Tomac's sister was an au pair, before she was siphoned off into the sex trade — we got a search warrant, and have found that the couple are Senhor de Garro's niece and her husband.'

'Ah!' Cannon said, 'another link.' He gave Maddern an approving nod as they reached the reception area. 'I've a bit more information on that score.'

The superintendent, CI Helen Moore and several other officers all stood as if regrouping for the next move.

'Have you a general call out for de Garro's car?' Cannon asked without preamble. 'He left here early this morning, with the contents of his safe.'

Cannon caught a swift movement of hand to mouth from an elderly woman behind the reception desk, who, when she saw his glance dropped her hand and stood up very straight, chin raised. Helen turned to her. 'I understood you to say that Mr de Garro had not been in today.'

She shook her head. 'No, he has not. I live in the flat next to his office, I would have seen him.'

'Then you,' Cannon said, 'will be de Garro's aunt.'

The officers instinctively spread and stepped towards her as a group; she stepped back just as instinctively.

'I think you both have things to tell us.' The superintendent looked at Cannon, then, nodding towards the receptionist, said, 'We'll talk to her in there,' and gestured to the office behind the desk. A policewoman and another officer stepped forward and persuaded the protesting woman into the office.

'It's Brand, the journalist friend of the first man murdered, that I'm worried about,' Cannon said, as the office door was closed,

255

'also that de Garro should not get away.'

'We do have a nationwide call out on his car,' Helen assured him.

Cannon related the window cleaner's story, adding, 'It's possible the van in the flowerbed could have been used to take Brand away somewhere. You should work on the driver, and there's a man they call the Vulture, with a badly pock-marked face. He's apparently de Garro's right hand man. He could have been the second man in that van.'

'We are already making appeals for sightings of this van during the last few hours,' Helen assured him. 'the trouble is there are a lot of white vans about.'

'Right, let's see what this aunt has to say,' the superintendent said.

'Your name is?' he demanded as his chief inspector and Cannon followed him into the office, where Cannon noticed the pictures on the walls were of local estates, houses and the health hydro. These, he was sure, would all be de Garro's properties.

'So let's put it another way,' the superintendent said when there was no immediate reply from the woman, 'Vasco de Garro is . . . '

'My brother, my good kind brother, who looks after all his family.'

'Your good kind brother has many business interests,' the superintendent went on.

256

'Yes,' she looked at him a little uncertainly. 'Yes, yes, he does, and he gives much to charity, many charities.'

'And he makes his fortune by?'

'Working, working,' her voice was rising each time she spoke and now she made expansive gestures of someone building higher and higher, 'as children we had nothing, nothing, and now . . . we have . . . ,' her hands reached to their highest extent.

'He made his fortune by exploitation and illegal practices,' Helen suggested, 'which you have helped to run here.'

'You,' she made a wide dismissive gesture, 'do not understand exploitation. We were exploited, as children we were exploited,' she shouted back,

'And you do not understand the law,' the superintendent said, 'take her away.'

The wpc and the other officer took the arms of the woman, who was now screaming at the top of her voice, that her brother was a good man and he would make them all suffer for this outrage. But her grandiose manner was fast evaporating and her lacquered hair had fallen down in stiff wings and flapped from its former faultless coiffure as she protested and struggled.

As she was taken away another officer came carrying clothes in a plastic evidence bag. 'We found these in a tiny room near those dogs,' he reported.

Cannon recognized the upmarket denim trousers and the pinstriped jacket. 'They're Brand's,' he said.

17

Cannon knew he could not blunder about in the dark, had heard that Bose would have a helicopter at eight the next morning, knew, for Helen rang to tell him, that they had found the man they believed to be the Vulture, picking him up at the railway station at King's Lynn.

'The man in charge of the dogs at the Hydro, who obviously thought more of his animals than of de Garro's right-hand man, described him to a T. His pock-marked face is more like a weasel than a vulture, but,' Helen paused before adding the bad news, 'the weasel's not talking. Will admit to nothing. We are still questioning him, and, of course, searches for Brand will start at first light.'

Liz was ready for bed in her pyjamas and had switched on the television in their sitting-room. 'No use thinking of going to sleep with all this going on,' she had said, watching with indifference as some creature with vampire teeth advanced on a victim. John stood at the window staring out into the blackness.

'Why,' he asked, 'do you strip a man before

you take him off in a van to get rid of him, to dump him?'

'A man feels more vulnerable naked,' Liz said. 'If they had tried to make him talk, and — ' she paused and he turned to see her frowning as she cut herself off.

'And?'

'They could have gone too far, he could have died because of whatever they did to him.'

Cannon thought of Brand's bull-like build, his constitution, his fitness and surprising agility. Murdering him would have to be deliberate, he'd take some killing by torture. 'No, I don't think so,' he said.

'Perhaps I'm just trying to prepare you for the worst outcome,' she said.

'Right, so now prepare me for the best: help me find him alive. Why strip a man off when he's not dead?'

'Well,' she began drawing in a deep breath as if for yet another effort at the end of what had been a long working day. 'Certainly if you'd strip him to make him feel more vulnerable, you are not going to redress him to dump him, and — ' She paused as a memory was triggered. 'What about the young woman we found who had nearly drowned in a dyke when her car slid in backwards? She nearly died of hypothermia, and, another thing, they could have taken Brand out in a boat.'

'But the window cleaner overheard the Vulture say they couldn't get things out to sea far enough, everything washed back in.'

'Yes, Hoskins said that too,' she reminded him.

'They wouldn't need to take him out to sea. He could just be dumped in a dyke, tied up and slid straight out of the back of a van into the water — at high tide those drains are deep enough to drown an army.' Cannon remembered the same girl's car swept away towards the sea.

'But at low tide often quickly exposed,' Liz said, 'and anyway why go to so much trouble? *And* I thought we were looking for him being found alive?'

'Explain, extrapolate,' John demanded.

'Well, DCI Cannon,' she answered the man who had reverted to rank, 'we know powerful rogues and their acolytes are usually clever men, often quite intuitive, particularly about each other. If this Vulture, this right-hand man, suspected de Garro was getting ready to run, why commit murder when all he has to do is make sure Brand is not found until he himself has got clear. There are plenty of places: old barns, the marshes, the dunes, upturned boats.'

He threw himself on to the sofa next to her, the heights of command relinquished. The vampire creature began to laugh maniacally; Cannon took the remote from Liz's lap and pressed the mute button. In the silence he once more mulled over the facts. The sheer weight and bulk of a man like Brand, plus his determination to avenge Nick, would not make him easy to handle — tied up, stripped, threatened at gunpoint, whatever. He had a sudden mental picture of Brand, in his underclothes, but as defiant as ever. There would be no embarrassment, no vulnerability, he was sure of that, and he hoped against hope that Brand was still alive.

The helicopter was going to be Cannon's best hope of directing any kind of search. He decided he would be at Northfield airfield well before eight, before light the next morning, ready to go with Bose. He turned to explain to Liz, but saw she was asleep.

He watched her sleeping. This had not been planned as any kind of retirement, just a different kind of service to the public they both enjoyed, but he so often seemed to leave the running of their pub to her, and he knew it was hard work. He was, he decided, a kind of maverick landlord. Could do better. He remembered it used to say that on his school reports.

Carefully he put one arm under her knees, the other under her shoulder and lifted her. She stirred, opened her eyes, laid her head on his shoulder and slept on.

He did lie down beside her, and though he did not undress, he slept for a time, but was up well before dawn streaked the sky. He crept downstairs, and was dithering because he did not feel quite right leaving a note, and he certainly did not want to wake Liz. She had been so tired she had hardly stirred all night. He dithered at the table, took paper from the dresser, stood pen poised, trying to find just the right words, when a voice behind him said, 'Just go.'

Liz, still flushed with sleep, pushed her long blonde hair back over her shoulders and shook her head at him, an admission she had no hope of ever changing him. 'Just go,' she repeated.

He took her into his arms, she was warm, reminding him of an egg collected straight from a nest. 'How can I bear to?' he asked.

'Let's face it, John Cannon, you haven't got time for me to tell you that. Go and fly that bloody helicopter with your new pal,' she paused, then was as determined as he was as he tried to hold her closer. 'Go find Brand,' she said pushing him away,

He broke the law and phoned Bose as he

263

travelled. The answer was that he was already at Northmarket airfield, but they were waiting for Cannon's briefing.

'Fifteen minutes,' Cannon said.

Bose met him and took him to the far corner of a kind of staff canteen, where mechanics and other workers were taking a break.

Bose introduced the pilot and navigator, adding that they were both local men. He was also introduced to a photographer who was up to his ears in a bacon sandwich but who cheerfully acknowledged the nickname Snapper with a nod, and a grin which showed each side the sandwich.

Cannon was irked by the cups of coffee and bacon sandwiches on the table, a casual breakfast, but knew time for this initial talk was essential, and he, after all, had only just arrived.

'We're leaving it to you as to where we should fly,' Bose told him.

Cannon wasted no time. 'My feeling is that this journalist has not been taken far from the Spa. We believe the owner and his headman are both making a run for it. The second-in-command was left to deal with a very inconvenient newspaper man after his boss had cleared out and gone, so we are looking for a place where Keith Brand, who incidentally is physically a big man, could be taken from the van quickly and secured for long enough to allow for a getaway.'

'We've already pinpointed the Spa,' the pilot pushed a map toward Cannon, his finger marking the spot.

'Right,' Cannon felt heartened, so they had not just been eating breakfast. 'I can't believe Brand would have been driven for any more than say up to ten miles — even that would seem too far if all you wanted to do was get well away. I feel the most productive thing we can do, is to first make an intensive search of this area.' He made an elongated oval shape over coast and dunes with the spa in the middle.

By the time they reached the helipad, Cannon appreciated that the pilot and his business partner/co-pilot were professional flyers. Snapper, a Jew with an engaging grin, no side, and probably no scruples, gave the impression that he had seen it all before, and had probably photographed it several times over.

'So we'll sweep the coast from Shepherd's Point and Snettisham south towards the Lynn estuary,' the pilot put names to points around Cannon's designated search area. His number two nodded as the rotors began to turn.

As they rose, Cannon looked down,

wondering what chance of success they had. The airfield slipped behind. Brand might not have been taken far, but he had been out all night, tides would have ebbed and flowed. The flat fenland was below them now. Luck was what he and this search party badly needed.

Two hours later, and a little hoarse from shouting at each other above the noise of the engine, they were flying a second run along the same piece of coast, this time more over the beach than the dunes and coastal strip, and low enough for the rotors to be stirring the waves near the shore.

Cannon was wondering whether he should now suggest they take wider sweeps away from the spa, when something caught his eye. He placed his hand on the pilot's shoulder, a pre-arranged signal for the helicopter to be hovered. Bose and the navigator glanced at Cannon who indicated straight beneath them. 'Tracks of a vehicle,' he said, 'straight into the sea.'

'Cocklers,' Bose suggested.

'Out of season,' the pilot said.

'Could you take a line on those tracks and fly straight over the water?'

Snapper, who was harnessed just inside the open door, lived up to his name and took several shots of the tracks.

The pilot nodded, turned the helicopter and this low they could clearly see where the vehicle had been driven in a curving sweep, until the tracks were now under the water.

'Tide comes in bloody fast over these flat beaches,' Bose said, and Cannon growled agreement.

They were suddenly alerted by a large black shape on one of the banks some hundred metres away. The pilot increased speed. Cannon tried to remember how deeply places like Seal Island and suchlike sandbanks were covered at high tide. Could someone stand up, for hours, and survive? He remembered holidaymakers with children being marooned in the summer, and having to be rescued by local fishermen, the fathers had stood with the children on their shoulders.

Everyone craned forward, then relaxed back with sighs of exasperation. 'Bloody seal,' Snapper said, but still clicked away.

Cannon put his hand on the pilot's shoulder. 'Could you go back inshore on the same line.'

'Follow the tracks back in, OK.' he shouted back.

As they neared the beach again Cannon had his hand on the man's shoulder once more, pointing over to the left to what must be the other end of the curving turn the vehicle had made. These tracks swept towards and then alongside an ancient breakwater.

The pilot did not need telling to hover, then to move slowly along above the blackened oak posts, which had probably been sunk in the sand many generations back to try to stem the force of the sea.

'There, there!' Cannon shouted, 'there.'

It took a moment for all to see what he had spotted. Something hung from the end post, the one furthest out, hung heavily, swayed ponderously with the incoming water.

'My God,' said Bose, 'I believe it is somebody.'

'Down!' Cannon demanded, undoing his seatbelt, 'I'll jump.'

'Wait 'til I say,' the pilot ordered, and the co-pilot turned and grabbed Cannon's arm. 'Shallow water, drop in gently, when you're told.'

Cannon nodded, aware of the danger of a broken neck or back from over-eagerness, but also certain from the size of the man in the water, his great head and bull-like shoulders, that they had found Brand. Whether he was living was another matter.

Snapper was working like fury, unaware of anything but his job, and swore, alarmed as Cannon pushed alongside him, spoiled a shot, and the pilot hovered and steadied some fifty metres to the right of the breakwater.

'Go!' the pilot roared.

Cannon hit the water, and the seabed it seemed, almost instantaneously, but not too hard, and he used the contact to push himself rapidly towards the surface. He was swimming before he reached the post. He tried to gauge direction so he came immediately to Brand's side, but the tide drove him past, with surprising force, further inshore and towards the wooden breakwater, so he had to fend it off or be crashed into it. Though once in contact with the structure, the soaked old oak felt almost an ally to his hands, elbows and knees, compared to the strength of this mild-seeming sea, and all the time he had his eyes on the body, the man, lashed to the end post of the breakwater.

'Keith! Keith!' he shouted. 'Brand! Hang on! We're here.'

He kept on shouting and just before he reached him he thought Brand moved, or was it just the extra aggressive wave that also banged Cannon at the posts?

He was nearly up to him, and could see Brand was gagged so tightly his jaw was forced back and down, with what looked like a leather strap. There were ropes and chains around his shoulders.

'Keith!' he yelled at the man, and like a leviathan coming up from the depths, waking from the dead, Brand raised his head. There was weed and sand in his hair and cold dark anger in his eyes, but Cannon rejoiced, he was alive, he had survived, survived over twelve hours in the sea, naked, bound, probably near drowned at the last high tide. Cannon knew from experience that it was the kind of blazing anger he saw in Brand's face that could keep a man going against all odds, but as he reached and touched him, he was icy cold, there was no time to be lost getting him out of there and to hospital.

To his frustration Cannon could neither undo nor move either the gag or ropes. He trod water and made signals as if using a pair of hedge shears back to the helicopter which had landed on the beach. In seconds Bose and the co-pilot were in the water on the way to him with bolt-cutters and a useful looking knife. He felt down the chains and found a padlock and a slight piece of slack in the links. Looking at the leather gag and the chains he wondered if they were from the spa's stock kept for their most lucrative trade.

He talked to Brand, who did not open his eyes again. Cannon kept his hand inside the slack in the chain, against Brand's icy thigh, and as soon as the bolt cutters were in his hand he slipped them over the chain at that spot, and closed them with all the energy of his own outrage.

At the same time as Bose cut at the gag with a pocket knife, the co-pilot sawed at the ropes with the larger knife, suddenly Brand fell forward, and even though Cannon was ready, he was pushed under the water by the sudden weight. The co-pilot hoisted him up, then took one of Brand's arms, while Cannon took the other, between them supporting and swimming with him to the shallows. Cannon thought Brand felt and looked like a mottled marble statue, like a sturdy Greek athlete, for the sea had left little of his underwear. It was also then that he registered that Snapper was in the water with them, with his camera.

By the time they reached the helicopter and had him loaded the pilot had informed the emergency services, police and ambulance. 'They'll be assembled at Northmarket.'

Brand was laid on the stretcher the helicopter carried and covered with blankets. He lay very still and Cannon hoped they were not too late, then as he tucked a second blanket around Brand's shoulder he opened his eyes and tried to speak and in a voice like a grated whisper, he asked, 'Have they got the bastard?'

'The one with the pock-marked face, yes,'

Cannon told him. Then asked. 'He did this to you?'

'Yes.'

They moistened his lips with a little water as Cannon added, 'de Garro, not yet.'

'Get him,' Brand said, 'tell my newspaper.' He turned his eyes towards Bose. 'Do the story,' he said, then looking at Snapper added, 'he'll have the pictures.' The effort cost him dearly, left him gasping, unable to get a proper breath. Cannon wondered if he was asthmatic, but finally and thankfully as they lowered on to the helipad the alarming spasm eased.

The scream of an ambulance siren reached them, and as they touched down Cannon could see it parking next to them, accompanied by two police cars.

The paramedics came aboard, gave oxygen and wasted no time making Brand more comfortable and secure, then loaded him into the ambulance. Cannon elected to go with him and was by Brand's side, the paramedic about to close the doors when Sergeant Maddern also climbed aboard. 'Well done,' he said to Cannon, 'and we've just found de Garro's car.'

'Where?' Cannon demanded.

'Edinburgh airport.'

Cannon looked down at Brand, who formed the word, 'go' with his lips.

18

'Edinburgh,' Bose repeated as he and Cannon stood together watching the ambulance drive away, Maddern now accompanying Brand to the hospital, as he had been detailed to do.

'So we assume this de Garro's flying out somewhere?' Snapper stated.

'Flown, I would think if he left the spa yesterday morning,' Cannon said.

'We should still get up there,' the photographer said, hitching the bag of equipment he never seemed to be without more firmly over his shoulder.

Bose nodded to him and Cannon had the feeling these two had worked together many times before. 'Now the story's broken the police should be keen to let us publish *all* the facts. They'll want the public on the alert.'

Cannon cleared his throat, but desisted from commenting that he'd known cases where newspapers had ruined any chance of prosecution after months of hard police graft. Instead he asked, 'Can we use the helicopter?'

'Under contract for as long as we want it,' Bose said.

'And no problem,' the pilot said, 'I know

some of the guys up there.'

'Fix it, would you,' Bose said then asked, 'meanwhile, where can we get some dry clothes.'

'It's not a big shopping complex, but there is a sports shop,' the co-pilot said.

'Right,' Bose asked the pilot, 'can you manage without your oppo while I take him shopping?'

'Yep, no problem, I'll be fuelled up and ready to go by the time you're back.'

When they did come back it was in a mixture of golfing and ski-ing gear, not individually laughable but all three together looked an odd bunch. 'Glad I didn't jump into the sea,' the pilot said.

Bose handed him a pull-on black and white diamond-patterned golfing sweater. 'Didn't want you feeling left out.'

Cannon was surprised at the authority and cavalier attitude Bose now radiated. He seemed to have forgotten he was retired, and a retired news editor at that, who presumably had not chased stories all over the country for years. He confirmed what Cannon was thinking by proclaiming, 'Let right prevail, justice for Nick,' he said. 'Let's go slay the dragon.'

As they rose into the skies once more, the photographer took a more active part as they discussed what they thought de Garro's movements would be. Cannon half listened to, and completely dismissed, his story of a car left near an airport as a blind, the suspect having doubled back on a train, until Snapper suddenly put his hand on Cannon's arm. 'You've been quiet a long time. What's your inkling?'

'I'm thinking about the luxury cruise line de Garro has an interest in, they sail in the Baltic, do the Norwegian coastal voyage. One ship was in Bergen, I remember, when we found out about the Buckansonn Line,' he turned to look at the other two, 'I wondered if there was a service from Edinburgh to Bergen.'

'I can tell you that,' the co-pilot said, 'KLM fly there, quite a regular service.'

'So are you thinking de Garro might be looking to board one of his own liners?' Bose asked.

'If there's one of them where he could reach it quickly, it's a possibility,' Cannon said.

'We can soon find out if there's one around Bergen,' Snapper said, 'I've got an app on my phone — we can do that now.' He had his slim black phone in his hand and was immediately stroking the screen to bring up the application he needed, then tapping his finger on icons and menus. 'Do you know the name of these ships?'

Cannon shook his head. 'Only remember the name of the line.'

'Not a problem,' Snapper said, 'I'll just do Bergen harbour.'

A few more taps and the screen changed from coastline to port, to outlines of ships.

'Not in the harbour,' he repeated after a minute or two, 'but I'll try these just outside.'

Three more taps and he raised a triumphant finger in the air. 'The cruise liner, *First Queen*, of the Buckansonn line, Captain . . . , well,' another flick of the finger, 'we don't need to know his name, or how many crew and passengers, but she left Bergen this morning.'

'So does it show where . . . ' Cannon felt a reluctance to even say the name of another of de Garro's boats with the word 'queen' in it.

'*The First Queen*,' Snapper supplied.

'Is now?' Cannon asked leaning over to see a torpedo-shaped image at a point beyond Bergen and a great mass of broken coastline and islands.

'She's not too far from Bergen, approaching the . . . ' he peered at the screen, tapped it to enlarge the details, 'a place called Ytre Sound, but if I know anything about these late cruises her next stop will be Trondheim.'

276

'Yes, I would agree with that. As a student I played guitar on some of the ferry-boats.'

'Do you know,' Cannon said, 'I can picture you doing that.'

'And we boarded some of these boats while they were underway. If one boat was not very lucrative we put off wherever we could, hired a fisherman or someone with a small boat and paid him to put us aboard another cruiseliner or one of the coastal ferries as they sailed by.'

'Sounds risky,' Snapper said.

'We were young,' Bose replied with that disarming *On Golden Pond* Henry Fonda smile.

'We're coming in to Edinburgh,' the pilot turned to tell them.

They leaned to the windows to see they were now in sight of the Pentland Hills which loomed behind the distinctive, empty-cotton-bobbin-shaped, control tower of Edinburgh airport. The helicopter veered to one side, to its designated landing site. Seeing the photographer easing his new trousers from his crotch, while Cannon felt his own were too roomy, he thought they might have been better to wait until they reached the bigger suppliers in Edinburgh.

The door to the arrivals lounge was opened for them, and they were met by a uniformed airport security guard and ushered through to a room behind customs where a uniformed police officer and a plain clothes officer waited for them. 'I have a message for you gentlemen,' he said, 'it is from Chief Inspector Helen Moore, who I understand is known to you, to say that we have confirmed that the man wanted has flown out to Norway and Interpol are on the case.' He paused to look at three blank faces. 'Is that clear to you all?'

'It is,' Cannon said, adding a belated, 'thank you.'

'There is also a message for a Mr Adrian Bose, who I understand is a journalist,' he said.

'That is correct,' Bose said.

'And Mr Walter Dub, photographer?'

Snapper nodded.

'The message is from your editor to say you are both to carry on with your normal duties.'

Not one of the three gave the least impression that this was anything other than a normal message, and the policemen obviously thought it was an instruction to return to whatever they were doing before they had diverged and come flying up to Edinburgh.

'Will do,' Snapper answered with alacrity. 'Normal duties, Mr Bose.'

Bose nodded. 'Indeed,' he said mildly.

That was it, and the three walked out of the room, braced, as if they still expected a heavy hand to land on their shoulders, but they reached the public areas and, as one, headed for seats at the nearest coffee stall.

'Well they're not following us,' Snapper said pulling up an extra chair for his equipment bag.

'I haven't had 'normal duties' for seven years,' Bose said, 'but by God I'm going to take them up again now.'

'Norway?' Snapper queried, 'we didn't ask if he flew to Bergen.'

'No,' Bose said, 'if we'd started asking questions, they might have taken too much interest in what we intended to do.'

'Interpol won't want us interfering,' Cannon added.

'But we go to Bergen anyway,' Snapper said, muttering something about having a nose for a story and this was it.

'Right, I'll go see if there are any seats on the next flight out,' Bose said. 'You're coming with us, of course,' he said to Cannon.

'I'd like to see it through,' Cannon said mildly, but his breathing was faster at the thought of being part of a chase to help catch one of the nastier pieces of humanity the world and man had created, a man who needed stopping before he murdered again. His innate prudence did make him pause to wonder about the possible financial cost. 'Of course, I presume your newspaper . . . ' he began.

'Of course,' Bose echoed, 'I need you, consider yourself on the staff.'

'I must phone Liz,' Cannon said.

'Probably best not to tell her where we're going.' Bose advised.

Cannon did not answer as he pulled his phone from his pocket and walked towards the front entrance to the complex. He would not imagine Liz would need much telling, she knew a lot of the facts, and no doubt Helen and Paul were keeping her up to date.

★ ★ ★

Liz had not expected her first customer that evening to be Archie Burns; neither she nor John had seen their absentee builder since he had called on the way to the airport to meet his daughter and their grandchildren from Australia. They had heard nothing more of his family troubles, or of their building work, since.

'Evening, Liz,' he said as he took one of the stools near the bar with a sigh of relief, then placing a folded newspaper on the counter he ordered, 'A half of bitter, please — no make it a pint,' he decided, putting his elbows on the bar and running his hands up through his sandy-grey hair. 'Well, that's that, then,' he said.

'That's what, Archie?' Liz asked gently, hoping the trauma of a broken marriage in the family had not brought some new tragedy, some terribly disturbed child, or a partner, unable to contain the emotional pressure, exploding in some act of violence. 'Not more trouble I hope.'

He looked up, shook his head, then smiled slowly. 'I'm tired to tell the truth, bone-weary. Just been to Heathrow again.'

'Your daughter gone back?' she asked, 'taken the children back to their father?'

'Well, next best thing, I've just picked our Joy's husband up from the airport. He's come over to take them home.'

'Oh so they are back together. I am so pleased.'

He nodded as he took a deep drink of his pint. 'I've come out of the way, wanted the wife to come with me, leave them to it, but she can't drag herself away.' He sighed. 'Well at least my trauma's nearly over,' as he spoke he unfolded the newspaper and turned the front page of the *Daily Endeavour* towards her. 'I picked it up at the airport,' he said, 'but you've probably already seen it and bought several copies.'

Liz wondered why she should think of doing that. The only picture on the front page was obviously taken from inside a helicopter, showing a man jumping out into the sea. An ancient wooden breakwater, lapped by waves, angled across a view of the sea. She peered, frowned. At the end of the breakwater was something — no, someone — tied to the end post. She looked closely at the broad shoulders, the bull-like head, great thatch of hair.

'That's the other journalist who went to the spa,' she stated, 'the friend of Nick's. Brand, Keith Brand, his name is,' she said.

'OUR CAMERAMAN WITNESSES A LIFE OR DEATH MOMENT'

'Was he saved?' she muttered to herself as much as to Archie, who in response reached across and tapped his finger on the man jumping from the helicopter. 'See who it is?'

She frowned, she did not recognize the falling, back-to-the-camera figure, arms raised above his head as he cleared the helicopter and was frozen by the camera-shot just above the waves. A secondary headline over the picture, read: 'Chained Up and Left to Drown'. The caption under the picture, read: 'John Cannon, a former Metropolitan police officer, was first in the water to rescue the second of our journalists to risk his life on this extraordinary story. Our first reporter was not so lucky . . . '

'John!' Liz's heart raced and she stood shaking her head at the knowledge that yes, of course it would be him doing such a thing. 'John?' she questioned, 'Where is he now?'

'That I can't tell you,' Archie said.

Liz was startled, had almost forgotten his presence and was running a gauntlet of conflicting emotions when her mobile rang. John's number flashed up. 'This is John now,' she said to her solitary customer,

'You go talk to him in private, I'll watch the bar.'

She pressed the reply button as she walked out to the kitchen, taking the newspaper with her.

'Liz . . . '

'Are you all right?' she asked first, and once she had that reassurance, 'What's going on?'

At the end of his reasoned explanation of why he could not possibly let Nick and Keith's ex-news editor down, and must go to Bergen, she asked him if he had seen that day's *Daily Endeavour?*

He hadn't. 'Read it to me,' he ordered.

She resisted the urge to say 'Yes, sir,' and opened to page three. 'It's a full page spread,' she said 'with pictures, more pictures.' She paused horrified as she realized the four shots showed the rescue in detailed stages. There were three men working to free the journalist: one cutting away a cruelly tight gag; John taking a bolt cutter to sever the chain; the third sawing through the ropes, and then Keith Brand, looking more stone than flesh and blood, caught in the second he was poised above the waves as he fell free. The extraordinary strip of pictures made her pause to admire the skill of the photographer.

She glanced now to the printed story and was again astonished. 'The first section is written by Nick,' she said, 'all about his chance meeting with Stefan Tomac at a motorway service station.' She scanned down the story and picked out extracts. 'The next part is by Keith, coming to Lincolnshire to find Nick . . . murdered . . . ,' she stopped: there was an aspect of this newspaper story and her situation, she did not understand. She glanced rapidly over the remaining section of the story. Was The Trap mentioned? It was not, but any newspaper man with any savvy would not take too long to connect the murder of a builder/journalist with this area, and this place, with its stables surrounded by obvious signs of building activities.

'Liz,' John interrupted her thoughts, 'I have to go.' He nodded his understanding of the tickets being waved at him by Bose from inside the terminal.

'You haven't said why Bergen?'

'One of de Garro's cruiseliners has just left Bergen. He could be on it.'

'Could be? Is that it?'

'Yes,' he said, 'I'll get back to you as soon as I can.'

'And not just on the phone, I hope,' she said.

'No,' his voice softened, 'not just on the phone . . . take care.'

'Take care,' she repeated to the dial tone, then turned hearing someone behind her.

'Paul!' she exclaimed, then saw Archie behind him. 'What — ?'

'Yes,' Paul said urgently, 'come on. I'm just ahead of the rat-pack press,' he nodded to the newspaper. 'I think every paper in the country is trying to get in on the act. I've locked the front door. Put your alarm on. The Trap, m'dear, is no-go until this news storm is over.'

19

From the air the coast of Norway looked so eaten into by fjords that it resembled a badly shredded brown and blue garment, and as they descended towards Bergen the setting sun flashed over a patchwork of glistening water and intervening land, backed by mountains with what Cannon thought might be the first snows of winter creeping down to lower levels.

They took a taxi to the docks and it soon became clear to him that the intention was to hire a man with a small fast boat to take them out to the Buchannson liner, and for them to board the liner as it cruised on its way to Trondheim. He looked at Bose; he'd forgotten he was no longer an investigative journalist, had he also forgotten he wasn't so young!

'Wouldn't it be just as good to go on to Trondheim and wait for the boat there?' he asked. 'After all we're only working on a hunch.'

'By the time we reach Trondheim every other newspaper man will be there,' Bose said.

'And Interpol,' Cannon guessed, if the

information he had passed to Liz was discussed with Helen and Paul, and acted on. 'If de Garro's on that liner he won't escape.'

'We'll just make sure,' Bose said.

'And be in there first,' Snapper added. 'It's our man who was murdered: it's our story.'

'If you want out, there's still time,' Bose said to Cannon.

Cannon shook his head, feeling a stupid, almost parental-like responsibility for these two men of the press. They seemed to be able to disregard most things, danger, common-sense, or conveniently overlook the law, in pursuit of their story.

Bose walked on at some pace, leading them along what he called the German dock of Bergen, a preserved section of the old water-front, where white, cream, golden and brown, steep-gabled houses, with only the narrowest of passages between, crowded the front, their bottom storeys now shops appealing to the tourists.

'There used to be several men with powerful boats who did all kinds of casual work, bit like the old London watermen,' he said and paused as several children, eleven or twelve-year-olds overheard what he said, nodded and waved.

'That is right,' one said, 'there is my father, Jan Render.'

As soon as Bose turned to the boy, the others crowded round, and Cannon soon realized their aim was to practise their English. They fell into step with the three men, and asked the kind of questions that sounded to Cannon straight from their classroom.

'What is your national flower?'

'The rose,' Bose answered. 'The English rose.'

'Oh! Yes, of course, thank you so much.'

'English is our second language,' another explained.

Ahead of them on the cobbled quayside a man stood hands on hips watching them approach.

'What day is your national day?' another asked.

'It is St George's Day,' Cannon offered.

'The twenty-third of April,' Bose added.

'What do you do to celebrate your national day?'

Cannon heard Snapper mutter, 'not a lot', but Bose was up to the mark. 'In country areas there are fêtes; games are played on village greens and there is Morris dancing, our Boy Scouts parade.'

'My son is not bothering you?' the man who had stood arms akimbo, inquired, coming forward to meet them.

'Jan Render?' Bose asked and the man bowed his head in acknowledgment. 'Your son has been very helpful. He says you could run us out to a cruiseliner.'

'Where is the liner? What is its name.'

The man was businesslike and the information given, he asked, 'You go now?'

'Yes,' Bose said, 'definitely.'

'Then quickly,' Jan Render said, 'before the sun sets.' He gave a wave towards the evening sky.

'How much?' Bose asked, and a small wodge of kroner Bose had acquired at the Bureau de Change Exchange before they left Edinburgh passed to the boatman.

Cannon felt mildly surprised they were not questioned about their ability or their right to board a liner during its journey, but perhaps it was part of daily life out here. There was no time to ask as the three of them were shown aboard a yacht, as businesslike as its owner. The engine obviously had plenty of power, Cannon thought, as it sprang into life and the boat had room for goods to be carried in its stern, along with enough seating for at least eight people.

He felt the enchantment and the beauty of this land overwhelm him as they left the harbour. He looked back at the multi-coloured houses, the green land behind the town, the mountains, and the snow. Some day he would bring Liz here for a holiday; in the spring, they could walk in the woods, along the fjords. Then he leaned over to look at the water. The sea here seemed to have a special quality, a kind of deep glittering blackness which promised an icy dipping if one should fall overboard. He had read stories of Second World War convoys to Russia, and the swift demise of sailors left in those waters for only minutes.

'How long to reach the liner?' Cannon asked.

'About one hour, or one and a half hour,' Jan replied from the wheel. 'They expect you?' he asked. 'I will radio for ladder to be over side.'

'I have an urgent message about the owner of the liner which must be conveyed to the captain of *The First Queen* in private and in person,' Bose said.

Cannon found himself trying to puzzle out which part of that message was not true, while Jan Render pushed out his bottom lip and nodded with great solemnity.

They were within sight of the liner after about three-quarters of an hour, and already the sun was low. He was wondering about Jan Render's return trip, when he heard the radio crackling, and a message first in Norwegian, then in English, and Render said, 'the captain wants to know if the message is for the owner of the line.'

'Yes,' Bose called back. It was a gamble and the three of them held their breath as the affirmation was repeated. Render listened out, and then switched off the radio.

'He will reduce speed and have the ladder out,' he said.

Cannon inhaled deeply, like a man preparing for action. So de Garro was on board.

'Thank God for that, on both counts,' Snapper said.

'Have you done this jump before?' Render asked.

One yes, and two noes, this time. Render pointed to just in front of the wheelhouse. 'You see the rigging set up there? I suggest you use that,' he turned to see them all nodding as he asked, 'who is fittest?'

The other two looked at Cannon. 'Me, I guess,' he said.

'And you have done this before?' Render asked Bose, who nodded.

'So you at the top,' he pointed to Cannon, 'you second, and the man with the bag at the bottom.'

'You must catch the ladder as I pass under the liner's bows, all three together, at different height, so as one you leave my boat — and I wish you well.' He grinned then. 'Don't worry, I will come back and pick up anyone who falls!' He roared with laughter, then pointed to where the liner was looming much larger on their horizon.

Very quickly, to Cannon's mind, they could read the name, and see two men lowering a rope ladder over the side they approached. Render gestured for them to take their place on the rigging.

Cannon thought he'd done some foolhardy things in his time, and was pleased Liz knew nothing about this, and that Snapper was too heavily involved and apprehensive, for even him to think of pictures. The little Jew was also far too encumbered by his bag. Cannon took it from him and slung it over his own shoulder.

'Thanks, I won't object to that,' Snapper said, then he caught Cannon's arm, with some alarm, for as they came nearer Render steered in a wide arc across the stern to the far side of the liner. 'What's he doing? The bloody ladder's the other side.'

'This is how they do it,' Bose reassured him, as they climbed into their places, 'he's going round under the bows to get in closer.'

'In front of the boat!' Snapper shouted. 'It'll mow us down.'

'It's a skill.' Bose shouted, but perched one

above the other conversation was now an effort.

Cannon felt he was at the top of the main mast of some galleon. It was much, much, windier than he had realized and he would have liked another reassurance from Render that he would come back if any of them fell — though would it be any use if he did? There were the liner's propellers to be thought of; he shivered and it wasn't just because of the cooling wind.

But the commitment was made and as they cleared the stern and raced up the port side of the boat he was not aware of breathing again. The yacht seemed to swing in under the bows, so close as to be suicidal, but Render caught the wash of the liner's bow just right and they were swept sweetly along the starboard side and close into the ladder.

Cannon remembered being pleased it was wider than he had expected, and the ribbed wooden slats forming the steps were broad. He jumped, then heard Bose yell frantically and furiously at Snapper. Below him the ladder jerked once, and after a thirty second eternity, twice. There was some cursing from the lowest point, but Cannon realized all three of them had made it.

Men on deck were reaching down towards him and he climbed up, feeling more as if he had been rescued from the deep than made a voluntary visit to this liner. The other two followed.

Snapper collapsed momentarily on to a hatch cover, but then was up and, taking his bag from Cannon, rushed to take photographs of Jan Render retreating into the dusk. 'Wave to him somebody,' he shouted. Bose obliged, and the returning wave was photographed. Cannon shook his head, as several of the holidaymakers who had witnessed nothing like this before, were also doing.

One of the sailors who had helped them aboard gestured towards the bridge. Cannon could see the captain watching from the rear windows. His expression even from a distance was clearly critical.

'This way,' one of the hands said, and led the way to a bridge which was a very different place to what Cannon expected. It looked more like a computer-room with a double bank of screens aligned around a raised padded seat, where an officer seemed to be steering the liner with controls that looked more suitable for a mobility scooter. Cannon in spite of their mission, and his need to confront and see de Garro under restraint, was fascinated. He wondered if the officer sitting in the driving-seat was following the red line he could see on a central screen.

Other screens seemed to show holds, stacked cargo, a thermometer on a hold wall.

'Captain William Mann,' the short stocky man, who stood feet apart, sure of his authority, introduced himself briefly. 'So, gentlemen, what is this all about?'

Bose glanced at the other men on the bridge.

'Use my cabin, sir,' a taller man with less gold on his cap brim offered.

'Thanks, number one,' Captain Mann acknowledged and turned on his heel adding, 'this way gentlemen.'

He held the door for them, saw them inside, closed it and went to stand at the small desk. 'Your request to board stated you have a message, either for one of the owners of this line, or about one of the owners of the line, which is it?'

'It's both really,' Bose began. 'We believe you have Mr Vasco de Garro on board.'

'No,' the captain replied, 'that is not the name of the owner we have aboard. We have one of the Mr Buckansonns aboard.'

'Could you describe him?' Cannon asked.

'Not much taller than me,' the Captain began, 'but broader, heavier, swarthy . . . or tanned . . . '

'Gold rings?' Cannon suggested.

The captain nodded.

'de Garro,' Bose said. 'Let's sit down, Captain. We have a story to tell you.'

He began, quickly handing over to Cannon, with Snapper fetching out his camera and bringing up the stored pictures of Brand being rescued.

'This man is in my cabin,' the Captain rose, 'but I am still not clear why you chose to come aboard as you did. Why not marshal the police and wait in Trondheim, my next port of call?'

'We're like an insurance policy, should anything go wrong,' Snapper said.

'Nick Eastabrook, who was garrotted, and Keith Brand, the man in the photographs just shown to you, were both my junior journalists when I was a news editor on the *Daily Endeavour*. My newspaper needs to make certain this man did not escape.'

The captain turned to the others.

'I'm a news photographer.'

'John Cannon, involved because — '

'The first murder happened on his doorstep,' Bose supplied.

'And he's a former DCI from the London Police and can't stand villains,' Snapper added.

Cannon was surprised at this succinct summing up, but as it fitted the bill, shrugged his acceptance.

'Well, I've accommodated the man you are

looking for in my cabin. So how do we go about this?'

'With caution,' Cannon said, 'he could be armed,' and added, 'I am fairly sure he'll recognize me — he stared at me for long enough when I went to his pub.'

'I'm told he has not dined, I could send a steward to see if he wants to eat in my cabin?'

'If he does, I could go in with the tray,' Bose said.

The captain vetoed that immediately. 'No, I think not, but I could easily go in saying I needed a chart from my desk. I'll keep him talking, then you can come in,' he glanced towards Cannon, 'and — '

'Make a citizen's arrest,' Snapper suggested.

'Well, disarm him,' Cannon said grimly, 'we don't want any random shootings. This man has a lot to lose. If we can just be sure he is unarmed and locked in somewhere until we reach Trondheim, I'd be happy.'

'Do we need more of my men?' the captain asked as he rose.

'No,' Cannon said, 'just you and me for a start.' He turned to Bose and Snapper. 'You two stay well out of the way until we've found out if he is armed.'

'So I go in, search for something or other in my desk.'

'And,' Cannon went on, 'the moment you select something, hold it up and say, 'Ah! This is what I'm looking for,' de Garro's attention will be on you, I'll come in and take him.'

The captain led the way to his quarters, clearing his throat, making no secret of his approach. He nodded to Cannon who stood pressed back to the wall, well out of sight, knocked briskly, then entered without waiting for invitation.

'Need something from my desk, Mr Buchansonn,' he said, adding, conversationally, 'Do you have everything you require? Something on a tray perhaps?'

'Sit down, Captain, I need you to do something for me,' de Garro said. There was a note in the man's voice Cannon did not like.

'Anything I can of — ' the Captain drew in his breath — sharply.

'If there is anyone outside the door, and I'm sure there is, would you tell them that I would like them to come in and sit down with us, and that they would be wise to do that because . . . '

'He has a gun pointing at my chest,' the captain said.

'And I shall use it,' de Garro said, then as Cannon walked into the room, he added,

'You again. I should have guessed the little boat wasn't a coincidence. You were around when my troubles started. It'll be a pleasure to shoot you,' he gave a brief laugh. 'Just give me cause,' then ordered, 'close the door!

'Captain, I need you to send a message to your bridge. I want the boat which has just dropped this man and two others off, recalled, now.' He waved the gun between the two of them and the intercom link with the bridge, then with disconcerting viciousness he kicked the chair from the desk towards the wall-mounted phone. 'You,' he said to Cannon, 'sit there, where I can see you both.'

Cannon did as he was told, watched and waited, took note of the small suitcase on the desk, which de Garro put his free hand on from time to time. Cannon had no doubt this contained the contents of the health centre safe, de Garro's cushion for his future — if he had one — if any of them had one.

The captain gave the order, then listened. 'No, the owner's request, and yes, as you ask, I have finished with your cabin, everyone should now be in their own quarters.'

'Now, we wait,' de Garro said, adding 'but make no mistake if I don't get off this boat safely I'll take a lot of people with me. I'll shoot every last one who tries to interfere.'

De Garro's concentration never waivered

as they waited — and neither did Cannon's. The intercom bleeped and the gun was gestured for it to be answered.

'The boat is nearly back,' the captain reported.

'Right, stop this boat.'

'Stop . . . this . . . ?'

'Stop this boat,' de Garro repeated, 'and remember I could fire two shots before either of you could reach me.'

The captain was clearly outraged at the idea of stopping his liner out at sea, but the gun gestured more forcefully to the intercom. 'There will have to be an announcement, or the passengers and the crew will wonder what is wrong. My second will be coming to my quarters — '

'Tell them to stop the bloody engines, and that you are under orders from the owner.'

It was only minutes before they heard the message being relayed through the ship, and shortly after that the vessel lost the deep rhythm of propulsion — noise that had hardly been noticeable before now left a vacuum.

The intercom bleeped again. 'Jan Render's boat is alongside again, sir, but he is anxious to be on his way back to Bergen. He wants to know if there are people to board?'

'Yes,' de Garro said. 'We will be right there.'

Cannon could see de Garro was sweating freely now. This was going to be the tricky bit: would he leave them below, lock them in, or attempt to take them with him, the threat of the gun concealed under his jacket. It was the casual bystanders Cannon was worried about. Then he was heartened a little as de Garro picked up the case — the man had that to encumber him and to worry about, and time was not on his side. He not only had to leave this ship, he had to give the police the slip, and disappear with his suitcase, once he was on shore.

'You walk in front.' The gun waved at Cannon, then at the captain, 'You just in front of me. I'll blow your back out first if anything goes wrong.'

As Cannon left the cabin the stillness seemed to him much greater than just the lack of engine noise. Wasn't this the time holidaymakers assembled in noisy crowds for pre-dinner drinks? Without turning his head or delaying on the way to the ship's side and Render's waiting boat, Cannon looked around as much as he could without too much head movement — and saw no one. No one, and the captain's words came back to him: 'Everyone should now be in their own quarters', he had alerted his Number One to the danger of the situation in front of de

Garro. Passengers had been advised to stay in their cabins until told, and the crew to stay well out of sight.

On deck the same solitude, all except for one brave soul who stood at the top of the rope ladder again deployed over the side. The man saluted the captain as they came near, and Cannon recognized him as the ship's Number One, but stripped of jacket and cap, standing in just navy jumper and trousers.

'You first,' de Garro said to Cannon, moving in behind the captain and no doubt pressing the gun barrel into the small of his back to remind him to make no unwise moves.

Cannon swung a leg over the side, and saw that the man securing the ladder at the bottom in Render's boat was another sailor. He caught Number One's eye as he climbed over, raised his eyebrows a fraction in acknowledgment that he appreciated the situation.

As he climbed down the ladder he wondered where Render was, below decks in the living quarters perhaps? Or had they taken him on to the liner? He also wondered how de Garro intended to deal with the captain as he came down into the small boat.

Then two things happened unexpectedly: de Garro shouted down to the sailor next to

Cannon. 'Catch,' he said and dropped the suitcase down to the man, who, taken by surprise, still managed to catch it, and place it by his feet, so he might steady the ladder for the next person down. Cannon also appreciated that once de Garro had them both on board this boat, and they were away from the liner, he would almost certainly shoot them. There were too many risks trying to watch three men, and maybe more if Render was below — and another two or three murders would be nothing to him. De Garro would then, no doubt, hope to deal with the last sailor when he was near to shore, probably going in to a smaller landing, a village with a single quay, perhaps.

But Cannon had not quite guessed it right. Above he heard de Garro shouting. 'Step back, right back,' de Garro was ordering, 'further, further!'

He realized the man had now drawn his gun and was waving it menacingly at the captain and his second-in-command.

Do as you're told, he silently urged them, and as de Garro stepped over on to the ladder still pointing his gun at the men on deck, Cannon knew what he had to try.

He moved without haste, stooped to pick up de Garro's case, then stooped again to try to put it down out of sight. A hand came up

303

from below, and Render took the case from him. It was accomplished in seconds, as de Garro left the deck of the liner and before he stepped into the small boat.

'Let go,' de Garro ordered the sailor holding the bottom of the ladder, 'and take me back to the coast as quick as you can.' De Garro moved to the stern of the boat where he could see them all. Cannon grudgingly admired the man's sheer nerve and quick cunning. To have got himself to this point of control took some doing, but Cannon waited for another moment he knew was coming, and as the engine of the boat was slipped into gear and they moved away from the liner, it came: De Garro missed his case.

Cannon saw his eyes flicker down to the spot where the bottom of the ladder had been, then the gun moved to him. 'My case?' he said. 'Where is it?'

'You mean this?' Render held the case up from below the steps to the galley, de Garro's eyes flickered to it and Cannon leapt, knocking the gun down as it was fired.

De Garro came for him like an enraged beast with hands clawed and going for the eyes. Cannon side-stepped and, using the force of the man's own rush helped him on his way overboard.

It was at this point Cannon realized that

the whole of the ship above him had come to life and the flash of a camera came again and again.

De Garro floundered in the water, sinking and coming up to shout, 'I can't swim!'

Render hefted a lifebelt into the water, and Cannon was about to dive in when Render caught his arm, 'It's roped, we'll just haul him in like a big fish.'

Any wish to do anything other than watch as de Garro panicked and threshed about in the icy waters left him, as he remembered another fish and the funeral he had given it. However, there would be no funeral this time, and just for a moment Cannon wondered if he really thought that was justice in this case.

Once they had de Garro back aboard the yacht was driven back alongside *The First Queen* where Bose would not let Render away until he had his full address, promised him a reward and Snapper had taken his photograph.

'Read all about it, eh!' Render said with gratification.

'The police will want to talk to you too,' Cannon called down to him.

Jan Render tipped his cap. 'Fine,' he called back.

Cannon, who had felt a little depressed when he thought of the long law processes to be gone through, was also cheered when later, over a dinner with the captain, Bose speculated as to what a long, long, incarceration would do to de Garro.

'His gold rings won't fit, that's for sure,' Snapper said.

20

All Cannon wanted to do was go home, but the three of them were kept in Trondheim for three further days by grim-faced international police, then hounded by the international press.

The number of pressmen had grown in Trondheim as news of de Garro's arrest, of the status he had enjoyed in the UK, of the variety of his organizations, and the scale of his crimes, spread. The press in every country in Europe seemed able to find that one of their own had been a victim. Then, with information of how many members of de Garro's own family were involved, the headlines became more sensational, labelling him 'The Portugese Godfather', 'The One-Man Mafia' and 'Murder! Keep it in The Family.'

Bose and Snapper were busy first on their mobiles and then on borrowed laptops, making regular contact with the *Daily Endeavour*. While they obviously felt the centre of the world, Cannon felt out on a limb.

They had no trouble at all contacting London, but Lincolnshire was quite another matter. He could have wept with frustration; just twice he heard a crackly Liz answer, realize it must be him, heard a static-laden question he thought was, 'Is that you John?' then nothing. He texted but got no reply, tried to email but the computer said all attempts failed. 'Hell!'

'Must be your Fens,' Snapper sympathized. 'Too flat to get a good signal perhaps.'

Then Bose came with the news that Brand was out of hospital and had gone back to The Trap.

'Lucky man,' Cannon muttered.

'Well, Liz will know you are OK *and*,' he paused for effect, 'we fly to Edinburgh this afternoon.'

'Thank God,' Cannon said.

They had not quite done with the media, for as they approached the Scottish airport they were requested to wait to disembark until every other passenger was clear.

'There'll be a car waiting for us,' Bose told them, 'we'll soon get away.'

They were escorted through the arrivals lounge flanked by security men. Cannon glanced at the horde of journalists and cameramen, all desperate for a new word on the story, or a shot showing a new emotion on their faces. He took a deep breath, lowered his head, and made for the exit doors, beyond which Bose indicated a waiting limousine. Unhampered by possessions (a carrier bag with some bought and some dirty under-clothes and a shirt, was all Cannon had), they were in the car in minutes, and all gave a sigh of relief.

'We have one more stop to make,' the driver announced, 'somewhere the media pack can't see, I was told, so here goes.' He swung the car the opposite way to the usual exit, saying as he did so, 'Whichever one of you is John Cannon, had better be ready for a swift jump out.'

'Now what?' Cannon exclaimed, his first thought was for goodness' sake, not another jump into the unknown! 'What's this about?' he appealed to the other two, but obviously they had no idea.

The car swept around the corner where a red sports car was waiting. The truth of the situation dawned on Cannon and he had his hand on the door-handle. 'Wait until I stop,' the driver warned with a grin in his mirror.

But he was out before they had stopped. Liz waved from the driving seat, but did not get out.

'Presume you're not coming with us, then,' Snapper said.

'We'll be over to see you soon,' Bose shouted, as the car door was closed and they were away.

Cannon ran to the passenger seat and Liz,

who had the engine already idling, drove too, but the opposite way. She joined the slow moving queue of cars leaving the airport by the usual route, unremarked in the crowd.

Cannon sat and looked at her profile, her hair, her . . . everything. Neither of them spoke until they were some distance from the airport and on a quieter road.

'Pull in,' Cannon said, 'there's a layby just ahead.'

'But — ' she began.

'Pull in!' he ordered.

She did so, but hardly had time to pull on the handbrake before he had reached across and taken her into his arms and kissed her heartily. He held her head tightly between his hands, swept the restraining band from her hair and let it free, then pushing his fingers through it, kissed her again.

'Better?' she questioned astonished by the suddenness of his actions, but her voice was soft. 'That was all — '

'All . . . ?

'Nice,' she said shivering. 'Flattering.'

'You're all right, forgiven me for going?'

'Ah, this is a different matter,' she said, looking at him, shaking her head. 'All I can say is that it is a good thing we have friends, who always step into the breach . . . or should I say — '

He reached over and kissed her again.

'So these friends?' he asked.

'Yes, Paul is resident in the pub, with Keith.'

'Brand? He is OK?'

She nodded. 'He says he can cook, so is in charge of meals.'

'Well, he did good breakfasts,' Cannon remembered, 'so we're covered,'

'Not only that, even the stable alterations are up and running. Archie Burns's got two more men and we're underway again.'

'A lot's happened in three days!' he exclaimed. 'You could say things go better without me.'

'I could,' she said, 'the only thing is there doesn't seem much purpose in any of it, without you.'

'No,' he said, 'and without you I'd . . . be nothing.'

There was a long moment's silence as they contemplated life without each other.

'Look,' he said, 'I've decided — '

'Never to do it again.'

'I've decided we'll stay overnight on the way home, have a break at Durham. There's a nice hotel there,' and when she turned to argue he added, 'you said the staff were capable. Let's speak to them, see what they say.'

A few moments later he folded the phone. 'It's easer this side of the North Sea,' he said.

'Paul doesn't mind?' she asked.

'No, old boy,' he mimicked, 'have a couple of nights while you've got the chance.'

⋆ ⋆ ⋆

They arrived at The Trap three days later, in the middle of the afternoon. Liz parked, then John unloaded the suitcase they had bought, and, with great show of it being the heaviest thing he had ever picked up, carried it towards their back door.

'You fool!' Liz exclaimed, laughing as first Paul, then Keith, came out to meet them.

All four laughed together, though Paul did ask 'So what's the joke?' as they both hugged and kissed Liz, shook John's hand and clapped him on the back.

'Rescued from the deep,' Brand said, 'always in your debt.'

'You OK now?'

Brand nodded.

'And thanks both of you for this break,' John said giving the case a flourish.

'So what is in there?' Paul asked.

'Very little,' Cannon said and grinned at Liz.

Paul put his arm around Brand's shoulders. 'We should just be glad they've come

312

back at all,' he said.

A short time later, mugs of tea in hand, they all wandered outside again to climb on to the picnic benches, lean with elbows on table, and breathe in the sea air.

'I'd almost forgotten what peace was like,' John said, 'no press, or at least not working.'

'Oh, make no mistake, journalists are always working,' Brand said, 'but you're fortunate. There's been the biggest jewellery theft ever in London, plus a rumour that something's happened to a section of the Great Wall of China.'

'Really!' Liz exclaimed and Brand shrugged his ignorance of any truth in the matter.

'What a blessing to be yesterday's news,' John said stretching contentedly.

That evening Paul and Brand insisted they finish their stewardship so Liz and John could either choose to be in the bar with their regulars, or upstairs alone taking just one more night off.

'Then we shall clear off,' Brand said. 'Paul's putting me up tonight.'

Liz was pleased to have an extra night to catch up with some of the neglected domestic tasks and have a general tidy round. John went down to the bar, and was sitting talking to the other two when they heard their first customer coming in. All three looked to the door.

'Who were you expecting,' Jim Maddern asked, 'the axeman?'

'Well, or Jones,' Cannon said.

Maddern sucked his teeth derogatorily. 'He's drowning in paperwork,' he said unsympathetically. 'But where's Hoskins? Thought he'd be here to help welcome you home.'

'He's busy with his houseguests,' Paul told him. 'The girl is crocheting throws for his armchairs. The old boy's like a dog with two tails.'

'What'll happen to them, that brother and sister?' Brand asked.

'They're anxious to go home, back to Porec,' Maddern said, 'though there's a little girl, just sixteen,' he paused, drew in a deep breath — this was just the age of one of his daughters — 'she wants to stay and live with her friend who works in a supermarket in Lynn. She's in hospital at the moment, but hopefully something can be arranged for her — eventually for all of them.'

Perhaps it was the thought of so many damaged lives, or the thought that if he stayed just sitting in his own bar he would be too available to be questioned about it to all, probably even the butt of querky humour on the subject. Cannon stood up quickly and said he thought he'd join Liz for a bit. He dropped a hand on the sergeant's shoulder as he passed. 'Good to see you, Jim.'

He and Liz didn't talk much, it was as if they both needed space and silence to help settle back into their lives. Liz went to bed well before the bar had quietened.

When Cannon heard the last customer depart and the front doors being locked he went down to see Paul and Keith off.

'Thanks again, both of you,' he said as they stood in the kitchen ready to leave.

'I may not see you again before I go back to London,' Brand said, 'but I will be back to see you and Liz before too long.'

Cannon nodded, they shook hands. 'If ever I'm in a tight corner I'll know who to send for,' he said.

'Me too!' Brand exclaimed.

Paul said he would be in the next day, but as he watched Paul's estate car disappear into the darkness, Cannon did not go straight back inside. He made a slow circuit of The Trap until he reached the spot from where the CSI tent that had covered the scene of the first murder had been visible.

'Rest in peace, Nick,' he said. 'Your story's been told.'

We do hope that you have enjoyed reading this large print book.

Did you know that all of our titles are available for purchase?

We publish a wide range of high quality large print books including:
Romances, Mysteries, Classics
General Fiction
Non Fiction and Westerns

Special interest titles available in large print are:
The Little Oxford Dictionary
Music Book
Song Book
Hymn Book
Service Book

Also available from us courtesy of Oxford University Press:
Young Readers' Dictionary
(large print edition)
Young Readers' Thesaurus
(large print edition)

For further information or a free brochure, please contact us at:
Ulverscroft Large Print Books Ltd.,
The Green, Bradgate Road, Anstey,
Leicester, LE7 7FU, England.
Tel: (00 44) 0116 236 4325
Fax: (00 44) 0116 234 0205

Other titles published by
The House of Ulverscroft:

THE BELLMAKERS

Jean Chapman

A heart-warming historical novel. Country life in the 1880s is difficult for three women without a man between them — and a living to make. As Leah seeks out her grandfather's debtors she encounters Ben and Nat Robertson, the bellmakers, and soon she and her faithful friend Ginnie become involved in a delightful summertime romance. But prejudice, superstition and gossip threaten to come between them, and the lust of a rich and determined man endangers Leah and those she loves.

MERCENARY

Paul Bennett

When Johnny Silver's brother, Carlo, the head of an investment bank, disappears — along with ten million euros — Johnny, an ex-mercenary on the run, is persuaded to come out of hiding to track him down. The trail takes Johnny deep into the world of gambling, prostitution, drugs and human trafficking, leading to a crime that shocks the core of a man who had thought he had seen everything . . .

A NARROW EXIT

Faith Martin

Detective Inspector Hillary Greene is due to retire in a matter of weeks. But her boss, determined to get her to change her mind about leaving the force, gives her a murder inquiry to handle. The victim, Michael Ivers, a gambler and a notorious womaniser, had few friends and there's a long list of murder suspects. Hillary has just days to find out who killed him — or her final case will be an unsolved murder. To add to an already complicated case, her old foe, ex-Sergeant Frank Ross is back on the scene — and a prime suspect . . .

TO DIE ALONE

John Dean

When the bodies of a man and his dog are found on the northern hills, Detective Chief Inspector Jack Harris and his team find themselves plunged into a violent world where life counts for little. The team is drawn ever deeper into the machinations of organized crime. Then as the fear grows that a ruthless killer is living in their midst, a second murderous assault rocks the hilltop community of Levton Bridge. As the mystery deepens, and people start to panic, the investigation reveals a disturbing world of secrets, half-truths and betrayals where lives and loves are casualties . . .

CRY BABY

Fay Cunningham

Gina Cross has a talent: she puts the flesh back on the bones of the dead, working for the police as a forensic artist. Gina is convinced there's a connection between the body of a teenage mother and a friend's missing sister. She enlists the help of investigative journalist Adam Shaw to help her find the missing girl. Their search eventually takes them to the mysterious Willow Bank hospital — which hides a deadly secret. But if Gina and Adam learn the truth about Willow Bank they may have to be eliminated . . .

MURDER IN MIND

J. A. O'Brien

As acting DI, Andy Lukeson had not expected to head up a high-profile murder investigation, but there he is, thrust forward into the limelight, investigating the murder of a woman whose death may be linked to a string of murders long unsolved. As he struggles to find the killer, Lukeson's fears of the case going cold haunt his every waking moment. Can he get to the heart of the matter before it's too late?